The Comfort of Saturdays

The Comfort of Saturdays

ALEXANDER
McCALL SMITH

Little, Brown

LITTLE, BROWN

First published in Great Britain in 2008 by Little, Brown

A CIP catalogue record for this book
is available from the British Library.

Hardback ISBN: 978-1-4087-0065-5
C format ISBN: 978-1-4087-0066-2

Typeset in Bembo by M Rules
Printed and bound in Great Britain by
Clays Ltd, St Ives plc

Papers used by Little, Brown are natural, renewable and recyclable
products made from wood grown in sustainable forests and certified
in accordance with the rules of the Forest Stewardship Council.

Mixed Sources
Product group from well-managed
forests and other controlled sources
www.fsc.org Cert no. SGS-COC-004081
© 1996 Forest Stewardship Council

FSC

Little, Brown
An imprint of
Little, Brown Book Group
100 Victoria Embankment
London EC4Y 0DY

An Hachette Livre UK Company
www.hachettelivre.co.uk

www.littlebrown.co.uk

This book is for Amy Tan

1

What made Isabel Dalhousie think about chance? It was one of those curious coincidences – an inconsequential one – as when we turn the corner and find ourselves face to face with the person we've just been thinking about. Or when we answer the telephone and hear at the other end the voice of the friend we had been about to call. These things make us believe either in telepathy – for which there is as little hard evidence as there is, alas, for the existence of Santa Claus – or in pure chance, which we flatter ourselves into thinking plays a small role in our lives. Yet chance, Isabel thought, determines much of what happens to us, from the original birth lottery onwards. We like to think that we plan what happens to us, but it is chance, surely, that lies behind so many of the great events of our lives – the meeting with the person with whom we are destined to spend the rest of our days, the receiving of a piece of advice which influences our choice of career, the spotting of a particular house for sale; all of these may be put down to pure chance, and yet they govern how our lives work out and how happy – or unhappy – we are going to be.

It happened when she was walking with Jamie across the

Meadows, the large, tree-lined park that divides South Edinburgh from the Old Town. Jamie was her . . . What was he? Her lover – her younger lover; her boyfriend; the father of her child. She was reluctant to use the word *partner* because it has associations of impermanence and business arrangements. Jamie was most definitely not a business arrangement; he was her north, her south, to quote Auden, whom she had recently decided she would quote less frequently. But even in the making of that resolution, she had found a line from Auden that seemed to express it all, and had given up on that ambition. And why, she asked herself, should one not quote those who saw the world more clearly than one did oneself?

Her north, her south; well, now they were walking north, on one of those prolonged Scottish summer evenings when it never really gets dark, and when one might forget just how far from south one really is. The fine weather had brought people out on to the grass: a group of young men, bare-chested in the unaccustomed warmth, were playing a game of football, discarded tee-shirts serving as the goal markers; a man was throwing a stick for a tireless border collie to fetch; a young couple lay stretched out, the girl's head resting on the stomach of the bearded youth who was looking away, at something in the sky that only he could see. The air was heavy, and although it would soon be eight o'clock, there was still a good deal of sunlight about – soft, slanting sunlight, with the quality that goes with light that has been about for the whole day and is now comfortable, used.

The coincidence was that Jamie should suddenly broach the subject of what it must be like to feel thoroughly ashamed of oneself. Later on Isabel asked herself why he had suddenly decided to talk about that. Had he seen something on the

Meadows to trigger such a line of thought? Strange things were no doubt done in parks by shameless people, but hardly in the early evening, in full view of passersby, on an evening such as this. Had he seen some shameless piece of exhibitionism? She had read recently of a Catholic priest who went jogging in the nude, and explained that he did so on the grounds that he sweated profusely when he took exercise. Indeed, for such a person it might be more convenient not to be clad, but this was not Sparta, where athletes disported naked in the palaestra; this was Scotland, where it was simply too *cold* to do as in Sparta, no matter how classically minded one might be.

Whatever it was that prompted Jamie, he suddenly remarked: 'What would it be like not to be able to go out in case people recognised you? What if you had done something so . . . so appalling that you couldn't face people?'

Isabel glanced at him. 'You haven't, have you?'

He smiled. 'Not yet.'

She looked up at the skyline, at the conical towers of the old Infirmary, at the crouching lion of Arthur's Seat in the distance, beyond a line of trees. 'Some who have done dreadful things don't feel it at all,' she said. 'They have no sense of shame. And maybe that's why they did it in the first place. They don't care what others think of them.'

Jamie thought about this for a moment. 'But there are plenty of others, aren't there? People who have done something out of character. People who have a conscience and yet suddenly give in to passing temptation. Some dark urge. They must feel ashamed of themselves, don't you think?'

Isabel agreed. 'Yes, they must. And I feel so sorry for them.' It had always struck her as wrong that we should judge our-selves – or, more usually, others – by single acts, as if a single

3

snapshot said anything about what a person had been like over the whole course of his life. It could say something, of course, but only if it was typical of how that person behaved; otherwise, no, all it said was that at that moment, in those particular circumstances, temptation won a local victory.

They walked on in silence. Then Isabel said, 'And what about being made to feel ashamed of what you are? About *being* who you are?'

'But do people feel that?'

Isabel thought that they did. 'Plenty of people feel ashamed of being poor,' she said. 'They shouldn't, but many do. Then some feel ashamed of being a different colour from those around them. Again, they shouldn't. And others feel ashamed of not being beautiful, of having the wrong sort of chin. Of having the wrong number of chins. All of these things.'

'It's ridiculous.'

'Of course it is.' Jamie, she realised, could say that; the blessed do not care from what angle they are regarded, as Auden . . . She stopped herself, and thought instead of moral progress, of how much worse it had been only a few decades ago. Things had changed for the better: now people asserted their identity with pride; they would not be cowed into shame. Yet so many lives had been wasted, had been ruined, because of unnecessary shame.

She remembered a friend's mother who had discovered, at the age of twelve, that she was illegitimate, that the father who had been said to have been killed in an accident was simply not there, a passing, regretted dalliance that had resulted in her birth. Today that meant very little, when vast cohorts of children sprang forth from maternity hospitals without fathers who had signed up to anything, but for that woman, Isabel had been

4

told, the rest of her life, from twelve onwards, was to be spent in shame. And with that shame there came the fear that others would find out about her illegitimacy, would stumble upon her secret. Stolen lives, Isabel thought, lives from which the joy had been extracted; and yet we could not banish shame altogether – she herself had written that in one of her editorials in the *Review of Applied Ethics*, in a special issue on the emotions. Without shame, guilt became a toothless thing, a prosecutor with no penalties up his sleeve.

They were on their way to a dinner party and had decided to walk rather than call a taxi, since the evening was so inviting. Their host lived in Ramsay Garden, a cluster of flats clinging to the edge of the Castle Rock like an impossible set constructed by some operatic visionary and then left for real people to move into. From the shared courtyard below, several cream-harled buildings, with tagged-on staircases and balconies, grew higgledy-piggledy skywards, their scale and style an odd mixture of Arts and Crafts and Scottish baronial. It was an expensive place to live, much sought after for the views which the flats commanded over Princes Street and the Georgian New Town beyond.

She had told Jamie who their hosts were, but he had forgotten, and he asked her again as they climbed the winding stairway to the topmost flat. She found herself thinking: like all men, he does not listen. Men switch off and let you talk, but all the time something else is going on in their minds.

'Fleurs-de-lis,' said Isabel, running her hand along the raised plaster motifs on the wall of the stairway. 'Who are they? People I don't know very well. And I think I owe them, anyway. I was here for dinner three years ago, if I remember correctly. And I never invited them back. I meant to, but didn't. You know how it is.'

She smiled at herself for using the excuse *you know how it is*. It was such a convenient, all-purpose excuse that one could tag on to just about anything. And what did it say? That one was human, and that one should be forgiven on those grounds? Or that the sheer weight of circumstances sometimes made it difficult to live up to what one expected of oneself? It was such a flexible excuse, and one might use it for the trivial or the not so trivial. Napoleon, for instance, might say, Yes, I did invade Russia; I'm so sorry, but you know how it is.

Jamie ended her reverie. 'They've forgiven you,' he said. 'Or they weren't counting.'

'Do you have to invite people back?' Isabel asked. 'Is it wrong to accept an invitation if you know that you won't reciprocate?'

Jamie too ran his finger across the fleurs-de-lis. 'But you haven't told me who they are.'

'I was at school with her,' said Isabel. 'She was very quiet. People laughed at her a bit — you know how children are. She had an unfortunate nickname.'

'Which was?'

Isabel shook her head. 'I'm sorry, Jamie, I shouldn't tell you.' That was how nicknames were perpetuated; how her friend Sloppy Duncan was still Sloppy Duncan thirty years after the name was first minted.

Jamie shrugged. 'What are their real names then? I need to know those.'

'Colin and Marjorie. And their surname is Macdonald. He's some sort of lawyer. Intellectual property, I think. And she . . . well, I don't think that she does anything, or anything for which she gets paid. She volunteers a lot. And she's very active

6

with a domestic violence shelter that looks after women who flee abusive men. She's always busy.'

'Why have they invited us?' asked Jamie.

Isabel hesitated, and then gave a non-committal answer. She had decided that the reason for the invitation, which was an unexpected one, was that the Macdonalds had heard about Jamie and wanted to inspect him. She knew that there had been gossip; Edinburgh was too small a place to allow a woman of Isabel's standing to take a younger lover without people talking about it. And some of this gossip had got back to her, as gossip inevitably does. The truth had been distorted, just as it is in a game of Chinese whispers. In one version Jamie was alleged to be a young sailor whom she had picked up at the Royal Forth Yacht Club annual dance, not an occasion she had ever attended; in another he was the gardener, Mellors to her Lady Chatterley; and in one particularly outrageous distortion, he was barely seventeen and had escaped from Fettes College, an expensive Edinburgh boarding school, to be with her. 'They said that he climbed out of the window,' she was told. 'After midnight. And that you were waiting for him on Inverleith Place, in your car.' In my green Swedish car, she thought; parked under a tree, in the shadows of night, the engine idling, waiting for a boy.

Had she been more sensitive to criticism, she would have smarted at these embellishments, but Isabel did not especially care what people said about her. She knew, too, that at least some of those who disapproved of her relationship with Jamie were envious; it is not always easy to accept the good fortune, the pleasures, of others. And anyway she had nothing to reproach herself for: she was barely into her forties and Jamie had just celebrated his twenty-ninth birthday. That was not an

7

impossible age gap, and was certainly no more than that which people accepted when older men took up with younger women. Nobody blinked an eye at that, and yet they judged women differently, and were only too ready to accuse them of cradle-snatching.

The Macdonalds were evidently curious to see what sort of young man she had acquired, and she did not resent their curiosity. In fact, she felt a certain pride in showing Jamie off; she had not set out to get herself a trophy, but if she had found one, then she might as well bask in the achievement. Trophies could be taken from one, be snatched away; she knew that. No trophies were permanent; they had to be given back, and perhaps she would have to give Jamie back, but not just yet. And not, she thought, without a fight.

There were six other guests. Isabel sat on Colin's left at the dinner table and on her other side was a cardiologist. Colin quizzed her gently about Jamie without appearing to do so. Isabel, impressed by his tact, gave him the information he was seeking: Jamie had a flat of his own in Saxe Coburg Street; he played the bassoon professionally and taught at a school; he saw a lot of Charlie.

'We live together but not quite together,' she said. 'It's not a bad idea to have one's own place.'

He nodded his agreement. 'Of course.'

'And he needs a place to teach.'

'Naturally.'

She waited for his next question. People had talked about Jamie being a kept man; they knew that Isabel had money and assumed – correctly – that Jamie did not. She must pay the bills. She must.

But Colin was too tactful. 'The old assumptions about how

people should live their lives – well, they've gone, haven't they? And there are plenty of options.'

Isabel smiled. 'I wouldn't write off the old assumptions too quickly,' she said. 'It may be that people are happier in conventional relationships.'

The doctor on her left had been listening. 'I'm not so sure,' he said. 'I've seen so much human unhappiness directly linked to being with the wrong person. It's as simple as that. People get themselves trapped. And that's the fault of marriage, isn't it? So many marriages are just awful. Long spells of penal servitude.'

Isabel turned to him. 'A rather bleak view, surely?'

'Realistic. And if reality is bleak, then I don't see what the point is in pretending that the bleakness isn't there.' The doctor looked at her challengingly. 'Or do you think otherwise?'

Isabel toyed with her fork. 'It depends. I'm not sure that I would deny the bleakness; but I'm also not sure whether I would dwell on it. Why dwell on something that will only make you unhappy? What's the point of that?'

The doctor drummed the fingers of his left hand on the edge of the table; a strange gesture which suggested, to Isabel, an impatient temperament. Perhaps he had been obliged to listen too long to those whom he did not consider his intellectual equals, exhausted patients with long-running complaints, unable to put their view succinctly. Some doctors could become like that, she thought, just as some lawyers could; prolonged exposure to flawed humanity could create a sense of superiority if one was not careful – and perhaps he was not.

'But most people are unhappy in one way or another,' he said. 'I found that out at the beginning of my medical career.

Most people are unhappy and afraid; all you have to do is scratch at the surface and it comes out.'

Isabel felt that she could not let this pass. And she had been right; he *was* condescending. 'I just don't agree with that,' she said. 'Not in the slightest. Most people are reasonably happy. They may not be ecstatic over their lot, but they're happy enough to carry on. Look at us in this room tonight. Do you think most people here are unhappy?'

She looked around the table. The dinner party was in full swing and the noise level had risen as a series of animated conversations got under way. There was laughter, candlelight and the glint of silver.

The doctor followed her gaze. Then he turned to her, his head inclined to allow for a discreet aside, although there was no danger of being overheard amidst the general hubbub. 'Happy?' he said. 'Do you really think so? When I look round this table I can identify three cases of extreme unhappiness. Yes. Three.'

Isabel said nothing, and the doctor continued, 'That man at the end of the table there is married to that woman over there. I take it that you don't know them? Well, he's having an affair with some younger woman down in London. His wife is furious and, naturally enough, very unhappy about it. He's unhappy because he can't go to London and live with his mistress because he has a business up here in Scotland. And a family. Bleak, I'd say.

'And then,' he went on, 'that poor woman on the other side of Colin . . .'

Isabel glanced anxiously to her right. It occurred to her that the doctor had drunk too much wine and become disinhibited.

'No, don't worry,' the doctor said. 'Nobody can hear. She's

called Stella Moncrieff. And you may have noticed that she's here by herself. She has a husband, though; they live in one of the flats down below. And right at this moment, I imagine, her husband is sitting down there by himself, thinking of what's going on a few floors up.'

'Why isn't—'

'Why isn't he here?' the doctor interrupted. 'It's shame. She goes out by herself. He's too ashamed to go anywhere. Nobody sees him any more. Never shows up at the golf club – he used to play off a handicap of four. Never goes to the theatre, opera, what have you – nowhere. And all because the poor man's ashamed of what he's accused of doing.' He paused and reached for his glass. 'Although I, for one, take the view that he's entirely innocent. He didn't do it. But that doesn't make things any better.'

Isabel was about to ask what it was that he had done when the conversation suddenly shifted. Colin, who had been busy with his neighbour, turned to Isabel and asked her about the journal she edited. 'Do many people read it?' he asked.

Pride made Isabel want to say that they did, but truthfulness intervened. 'Not many,' she said. 'In fact, sometimes we publish papers that I suspect next to nobody reads.'

'Then why publish them?' asked the doctor.

Isabel turned to him. 'A simple utilitarian reason,' she said evenly. 'Because it adds to happiness. In a very small way, but it does.' She paused. 'And then, there are some conversations that may have very few participants, but which are worth having anyway.'

The doctor stared at her for a moment, and then looked down at his plate. On the other side of the table, Jamie caught Isabel's eye; his look flashed her a message, but she could not make out what it was. It might have been *Help*, but then it might equally have been *What are we doing here?* Of one thing, though, she was certain: it was not *I'm enjoying myself*.

The doctor, looking up, witnessed the exchange, and threw a quick glance at Isabel.

'That's Jamie,' whispered Isabel. 'He's here with me. And I can assure you that if he's unhappy it's a purely temporary condition.'

2

'Ramsay Garden,' said Isabel.

'Gardens,' corrected Grace, her housekeeper. Grace was punctilious in all matters and would not hesitate to point out mistakes, whether made by her employer or by anybody else. She was particularly fond of correcting politicians, whose pronouncements she weighed with great care, searching for inconsistencies – and for half-truths – of which she said she found many.

This time she was wrong. 'Actually it's Garden,' said Isabel. 'Singular. Probably because the houses were built up around a small garden.'

Grace was glowering at her, but Isabel continued, 'Mr Ramsay's garden, no doubt. The poet, that is, not his son the painter. He had a house there, I understand. He came to Edinburgh as a wig-maker and did extremely well. Then he became a bookseller and his son became an artist.'

Grace was tight-lipped. 'I see.'

They were in the kitchen of Isabel's house, Grace having just arrived for work. She had found Isabel at the table, the *Scotsman* crossword in front of her, a cup of coffee beside it.

Grace regarded crosswords as a form of addiction, to be handled with the same caution as alcohol, and in her eyes to do a crossword so early in the morning seemed akin to taking a glass of whisky with breakfast. And now, of course, there were sudokus, an even more dangerously addictive pursuit, although she had not seen Isabel stray over to them just yet.

There was no sign of Charlie, apart, that is, from a small red fire engine and an already-battered stuffed bear propped up against the leg of a chair. His absence, though, was quite normal: Charlie was a child of habit, and he awoke every morning at five forty-five more or less exactly. Isabel would give him his breakfast and play with him for precisely two hours, at which point, with the same regularity with which Immanuel Kant took his daily walk in Königsberg, Charlie would begin to yawn. By the time Grace arrived he would be sound asleep, and would remain in that state until nine thirty, when he would wake with a hungry howl.

Isabel had adjusted remarkably quickly to these early starts to the day. She reminded herself that there were parents whose day began much earlier. At the informal mothers and toddlers group that she attended at the coffee bar at the top of Morningside Road, there was a mother who was wakened each morning at three by a hyperactive son; she did not have to contend with that at least. And there was another respect in which she knew that she was inestimably privileged. She had Grace to help her with Charlie during the day, and Jamie, of course, to help her in the evenings. And when it came to babysitting, as it had the previous night, there was a sixteen-year-old girl further down the street who was always available and keen to earn a little pin money. Nobody else in the mothers and toddlers group was in that position, and so Isabel was discreet; Grace had never been mentioned in that company, although, if asked, Isabel would have admitted that she had help. Wealth, she thought, was something that should not be flaunted – even indirectly – but one should not lie.

'And did you enjoy it?' Grace asked, moving to the sink, where a few cups had accumulated.

'Oh, it was the usual sort of dinner party,' Isabel said. 'A fair amount of gossip. Chit-chat. And we didn't particularly enjoy it. In fact, Jamie didn't enjoy it at all.'

She looked at Grace, and found herself wondering whether the other woman ever had meals with friends. Grace lived by herself; there had been a man, some time ago, but he was never mentioned, and Isabel realised that she did not want to talk about him. Once, only once, had Grace mentioned him, and had been on the point of saying more, but tears had intervened and the subject was dropped. He had been unfaithful, Isabel assumed, or merely indifferent perhaps; hearts can be broken in so many different ways.

Grace had friends, but Isabel was not sure whether they were the sort to meet one another for dinner; somehow she thought they were not. Many of these friends, although not all, were members of the spiritualist circle to which Grace belonged, and Isabel felt as if she knew them from the accounts which Grace gave of their meetings. The previous evening, for instance, when she and Jamie had been at the dinner in Ramsay Garden, Grace had been at a spiritualist meeting, and one of her friends, Georgina, had received a message.

'I know that you have your doubts about it,' Grace informed Isabel, as she began to load the dishwasher. 'But there was a very good medium at the meeting last night. A man from Lerwick, a Shetlander. You don't often get mediums from up

15

north. It's the first time, in fact, that we've had anybody from the Shetland Islands – or even from Orkney.'

Isabel had heard about Georgina, who looked after an aged mother in Leith and whose husband had died on a North Sea oil platform. There had been an explosion, Grace had told her, and Georgina had been left alone with her aged mother. It was the explosion, Isabel imagined, that had begun the path that led to the spiritualist meetings and the quest for a message from the other side. The other side – that was what Grace called it, although Isabel preferred the other shore, if one were to have an expression for a place whose existence was debatable. How crowded that shore must be, and how lost the wraiths upon it, jostling one another, waiting for some ghostly ferry; but she immediately reproached herself for the thought. If people needed to believe in the existence of another shore, then who was she to deny them that comfort? And Isabel had enough humility to recognise that there might come a time when she would take comfort in just such language and precisely such a notion. Perhaps that time had already come; if the miracle of Charlie had done anything for her, it had made her more convinced that a life without a spiritual dimension – whatever form that spiritual dimension took – was a shallow one. Not that this would ever induce her to await a message from one of Grace's mediums . . .

'And this man – this Shetlander – had a message for Georgina?'

Grace nodded. 'He did.'

Isabel looked down at the crossword. *A timely spirit?* Zeitgeist, of course. Another coincidence.

'What did he say? Anything specific?'

When she replied, Grace's tone was cagey. 'He said quite a

bit. There was somebody on the other side who had seen her husband. That was the message.'

Isabel's eyes widened. 'Seen him? In the flesh?' She could not help wondering: if the husband had died in an explosion, then what if . . . what if he was not all there? Or did the bits come back together again on the other side?

Grace sighed. 'The other side is part of the spirit world,' she said. 'I did tell you, you know. We don't have the same form once we've crossed over.'

Isabel wondered how people recognised one another if they did not have the same form. Or did knowledge in that dimension not depend on the senses? She wanted to ask Grace about this, but the words died on her lips. Her question would not sound serious, however careful she was in the framing of it, and Grace, who was sensitive on these matters, would take offence, would become taciturn. It was just too easy to poke fun at spiritualist beliefs; Madame Arcati and her blithe spirits never seemed far away, with their knocking once for yes and twice for no and all their Delphic predictions.

She folded up her newspaper and rose to her feet. As editor, and now owner, of the *Review of Applied Ethics*, Isabel was free of the tyranny of office hours, but she was conscientious to a fault. She had worked out that the editing of the journal and all the correspondence this entailed took about thirty hours of her time each week. That did not amount to a full-time job, but it was close enough, and it did mean that if she took a day off she would notice it in the resulting build-up of work. So she stuck to a pattern of working for at least three hours every morning and two hours in the afternoon or evening. Of course there were weeks when she worked much more than that, particularly in the couple of weeks before the publication

17

of an issue – the *Review* was a quarterly – when last-minute editing or proofreading issues inevitably arose. Then the button was eventually pushed and the *Review* went to print. Isabel liked the expression that newspaper journalists used: they put the paper to bed. It was a comfortable, maternal metaphor, she felt, and she imagined herself tucking a set of proofs under the sheets and kissing it goodnight. Children had that warm, freshly bathed bedtime smell; the *Review* would smell of ink, she thought, when she put it to bed.

Grace turned round from the sink. 'You're working this morning?'

'I have to,' said Isabel. 'I'll take Charlie out this afternoon.'

It was the usual arrangement. Grace had welcomed the arrival of Charlie just over sixteen months ago, and although they had never formalised things, she had expanded her job to include helping with him. This suited both of them very well. For Grace, it was the chance that she herself had never been given to play a part in bringing up a child, and the fact that she had become besotted with Charlie also helped. For Isabel, it meant not only that she could get on with her work, but also that the time she spent with Charlie was unaffected by the sheer exhaustion that a small child can visit upon his parents.

'I'll take him down to the canal,' said Grace. 'He loves the boats. Maybe he'll become a sailor when he grows up.'

Isabel frowned. Charlie would not be a sailor. He would be . . . Her frown turned into a smile. There were mothers, she assumed, who marked their children down for a career when they were still babes in arms, just as in the past they had promised children in marriage. Of course hardly anybody did that now, but we still worked hard enough to make sure that our children turned out reasonably like ourselves. We enrolled them in religions; we made them learn musical instruments we ourselves would have liked to play; we burdened them with family names. And here she was thinking that Charlie would not be a sailor, because being a sailor had not been on her agenda for him. But he might *want* to be a sailor . . .

'Yes,' said Isabel. 'Perhaps he will be a sailor. Anything is possible.'

'But not a soldier,' said Grace.

Isabel agreed. Charlie would never be a soldier. He would be far too gentle for that. He would be like his father, like Jamie. He would be musical. He would be gentle. Jamie could never point a rifle at anybody, she thought, even if they deserved it – as one's enemies always did, of course.

Then Grace muttered: 'I was in love with a soldier once.'

Isabel, on the point of leaving the room, stopped in her tracks; a soldier had never been mentioned before. She waited for Grace to say something more, but she did not, and continued with her work at the sink in silence.

The morning post had arrived. Isabel collected it as she left the kitchen on her way to the study, scooping up the envelopes that the postman had stuffed through the front door. She could tell at a glance that there was nothing personal in the mail, and that just about everything was for the *Review*. She noticed a bill from the printer and a letter from Jim Childress at the University of Virginia; the remaining six items were manuscripts from prospective authors. These she would look at that morning and, if they were worth sending for peer review, she would dispatch them in the afternoon post. The rest would be returned to their authors, but only after a few days had elapsed; it would be rude to send them back the same day – authors looked at postmarks and were always ready to detect cavalier rejection. Of course, Isabel would not reject anything groundlessly; she read each paper and gave it the consideration it deserved. But even then, there were some papers that were just so amateurish or, in certain cases, so clearly the product of delusion or paranoia that there was no point in reading beyond the first page or two. She handled these carefully, since on more than one occasion the author of such a paper had become threatening, even if only from a distance.

She went into her study and set the bundle of envelopes down on the table. There had been a run of fine weather and the morning was a warm one; even her study, on the wrong side of the house for the morning sun, seemed hotter than usual, and Isabel crossed the room to open a window. As the heavy Victorian casement slid upwards, the outside air rushed in, carrying the smell of freshly mown grass from the neighbouring garden, and perhaps the slightest trace of something else: flowering gorse, possibly, or blown roses.

She stood in front of the open window for a moment, feeling the flow of air over her bare arms. Who was it who stood naked in front of an open window, even in winter, and took what he called his 'air bath'? She had to search her memory for a good minute or so before the answer came: Lord Monboddo, the eighteenth-century judge and philosopher; he who, in his curious way, predicted Darwin, but was ridiculed for his insistence that men once had tails. She liked the idea of an air bath; she liked breezes and winds, she found them interesting. *The winds must come from somewhere when they blow* . . . The haunting line of Auden came back to her – WHA, of course. Yes, the winds came from somewhere – but that was not the point of the observation; the point was there were mysteries that we could not solve, answers we could not give.

She returned to her desk and to the task of dealing with the pile of mail. She extracted Jim Childress's letter and read it first; it was a quirk of hers to read first those letters she looked forward to receiving, leaving the least welcome to last. Jamie had noticed this and suggested that she should do it the other way round, but Isabel had pointed out that irrational habits were exactly that – irrational.

She read what Jim had to say. She had asked him to review a book, and he had agreed but had proposed a review article, which he said the book merited. Isabel would agree to that, of course. Then there was the bill from the printer – quickly dealt with – and after that, the manuscripts.

The first two were unexceptional. A recent book had raised the issue of why the genetic enhancement of human beings was wrong and had argued that this was because human nature was a gift; one should not renegotiate a gift. The first paper took exception to this, arguing that there were other, more powerful reasons for not interfering in our genes. Isabel read the paper quickly and looked up at the ceiling. She felt uncomfortable at the thought of people enhancing themselves, becoming supermen and superwomen. But why? People educated themselves and went to the gym to do precisely that – to improve themselves intellectually and physically. If that was acceptable, then what was wrong with doing it through genetic engineering in the womb? Perhaps the answer lay in the motives of the people who would want to do that. They would do it to be better than the rest of us, to have an advantage. But any athlete, striving towards physical perfection, was motivated by exactly that; so it was all about *selective* egalitarianism, thought Isabel.

That paper would certainly be sent to referees for review, and she hoped that they would recommend publication. Then the second paper, a rather dull article about good Samaritanism – again that would be sent to reviewers even though it lacked any discernible passion. It was a tenure piece, she thought; some poor untenured professor somewhere in an obscure university needed a publication or two to keep his job. Well, that was one of the ways in which the *Review of Applied Ethics* could make the world a better place, at least for untenured professors of philosophy.

She slit open the third envelope and noticed immediately the headed paper of the accompanying letter. She drew in her breath and read quickly to the bottom; there was the signature, bold as brass: Christopher Dove. She read the letter again, more slowly this time.

Dear Ms Dalhousie,

I enclose with this letter an article that I have recently completed and that I think is suitable for publication in the *Review*. You may be familiar, of course, with the famous Trolley Problem that Philippa Foot raised all those years ago in *Virtues and Vices*. I have recently given this matter considerable thought and feel that I have a new approach to propose. There are a number of other editors keen to take this piece (both here and in the United States), but I thought that I would give you first option. I do this because I am keen to show that there is no ill will – on my part at least – in respect of the way in which I was treated last year.

I would be grateful if you could let me know as soon as is convenient – and certainly within the next three weeks or so – as to whether you wish to publish this article. Sorry to rush you, it's just that I am under some pressure from the other journals to let them run it, and it would be kind not to keep them waiting too long. I'm sure you understand.

Yours truly,

Christopher Dove

She put the letter down on the table, noticing as she did so that her hand was shaking. Isabel had no colleagues – a consequence of being the only editor and sole proprietrix of the *Review* – so there was nobody she could turn to and say, as one does in an office, Take a look at this or Would you believe this? She wanted to do something like that now, but could not, and so she contented herself with a sharp exhalation of breath, a cross between a sigh and a gasp, which may have sounded odd but expressed perfectly what she felt at that moment. Then she picked up the letter again and began to enumerate its various effronteries and, not to beat about the bush, lies.

To begin with, there was Dove's choice of the words *you may be familiar with*, which may have sounded innocuous, but was in reality a piece of naked condescension. Of course she would be familiar with the Trolley Problem, one of the most famous thought experiments of twentieth-century philosophy – and twenty-first-century philosophy too, since the problem continued to rumble along, as everyone knew. Everyone professionally involved in philosophy, that is, and that included Isabel. To suggest that she *may* be familiar with it was to imply ignorance on her part; what Dove ought to have written was *you will of course be familiar with*. That was the principal insult.

Then there was the lie. Dove said that his paper was being sought after by other editors, but how could he say that, given

23

the strong convention that one did not submit the same paper to more than one journal at the same time? And even if he had, and one or two other editors had accepted it, then why would he now submit it to her? It might be that he considered the *Review of Applied Ethics* to be more prestigious than the other journals involved, but if that were the case, then surely he would have submitted it to the *Review* first, or at least simultaneously. No, Dove was lying, and the reason for his lie was that he was trying to *bounce* Isabel into accepting an article that was much sought after. Well, she thought, I will not be bounced.

Finally, there was Dove's sally about having been treated badly in the past. It was true that Isabel had dismissed him from the editorial board, along with his co-plotter, the ridiculously named Professor Lettuce, but she had done so only because he and Lettuce had conspired to remove her from the editorship. That was why she had decided to buy the *Review* and clean the Augean stables. So he was in no position to claim that he had been treated badly; the composition of her editorial board was entirely up to her, and she had decided that it would include neither Dove nor Lettuce. They had been informed of this decision and thanked for their past contribution; as conspirators they could hardly complain.

She turned to the paper which accompanied Dove's letter: 'Taking the Trolley One Stop Further: A Re-examination Along Different Lines'. Now that, thought Isabel, is a mixed metaphor: stops and lines were different features of trolley systems, and it was confusing to bring them both in. Dove was trying to be clever in an elegant, post-modern way, but she was not impressed.

She turned the page and read the page-long summary that followed.

'A trolley car,' wrote Dove, 'is careering out of control down a slope. Ahead of it on the line are five people who have been tied there by a mad philosopher. You, however, realise that by flicking a switch you can divert the trolley on to a spur line. There is one person standing on the line. If you flick the switch, one person will be killed; if you do nothing, five will die. Do you flick the switch?'

I have never had any doubt as to what I would do, thought Isabel. I would flick the switch. It was perfectly simple. Unless, of course, Dove and Lettuce were among the five . . . She stopped herself. That was an uncharitable thought, and she ought not to think it. But the delicious, childish fantasy came back.

'It is not so simple,' Dove continued. 'Since Philippa Foot first posed the problem, a number of writers have examined it in greater detail, most notably Judith Jarvis Thomson, who changed the conditions of the thought experiment by taking out the spur line and introducing an innocent fat man. This fat man is on a bridge directly above the trolley line. If he is toppled from the bridge directly in front of the trolley, his bulk will be sufficient to stop it and therefore save the five people further down the line.

'For many, that changes the nature of the problem, in that the fat man was never at risk until you toppled him over the parapet. Your intervention there is different from your intervention in flipping the switch. In this paper I explore that distinction and introduce another complication: the fat man is not innocent at all, but a serial killer who has a good few years of murder ahead of him. Does this make it easier to throw him over the bridge?'

Yes, thought Isabel. Of course it does. I would not hesitate to throw a serial killer off a bridge, provided I was sure that this was the only way of stopping him. For a moment she imagined herself locked in a struggle with a fat man on a bridge, in much the same way as Sherlock Holmes wrestled with Moriarty above the Reichenbach Falls. Holmes toppled over, and she feared that she would too, which was not the way the thought experiment was meant to end.

'No,' Dove went on. 'We have no right to take upon ourselves a god-like power to save the lives of others. In this paper I examine why this almost counter-intuitive conclusion is right.'

Isabel flicked through the pages that followed. Here and there a phrase caught her eye: 'we must respect the moral luck of others', and 'moral desert cannot be allowed to determine life-and-death decisions'. Oh, can it not? thought Isabel. She, for one, disagreed with that profoundly. We did not all have an equal right to life; she would have no compunction in saying that those who did some good for humanity should be preferred when it came to saving lives. If she was in a lifeboat and had only one place available, she would reach out to rescue Mother Teresa rather than Idi Amin, if both nun and dictator were in the water at the same time. And Mother Teresa, had she been in the boat, would surely make a similar choice, if she were faced with a drowning Idi Amin and a vaccine-research scientist. She would regret it, no doubt, and express sympathy for the floundering dictator, but surely she would do it.

She laid the paper down on her desk. The dilemma of the bystander at the switch was a difficult one, but there were other situations which seemed every bit as uncomfortable, even if they did not involve issues of life and death. And amongst these was the immediate question of what she should do with Dove's paper. If she were petty, she would send it back to him with a straightforward rejection. She might even say something cutting, such as, I regret that your paper does not meet the exacting standards of the *Review*. I do hope that you find another home for it. But that would be so cheap, so childish. No, she would have to send it out to referees, and at the end of the day she felt that she would have to publish it. If she did not, then Dove would have proved his point and would conclude that she had been swayed in her editorial decision by personal animosity towards him. She would not let that happen; Dove would be treated in exactly the same way as any other person who submitted a paper to the *Review*. He would be given equal treatment, which is exactly what he deserved.

Sometimes, thought Isabel, it is very difficult being a philosopher. How much easier it would be to be Jamie, who did not agonise over things, or Grace, who largely accepted things, or even Charlie, who did not yet know what things were.

3

Isabel did not see Jamie that evening. There was an unspoken understanding between them that he would be in charge of Charlie's bath and they would both then share the hour or so of play that came before bedtime. Then she and Jamie would have dinner together, going over the day's events, discussing Charlie and his doings and achievements, which were as wondrous to both of them as such things always are to parents. That evening, though, Jamie was involved in a rehearsal for a concert that he was to play in the following night at the Queen's Hall, and that was where she was to see him next.

On the evening of the concert, she found him in the Queen's Hall bar, sitting at a table by himself, nursing a large glass of orange juice and paging through an opera magazine. He rose to greet her, and they exchanged a kiss on the cheek. His hand, though, touched the side of her neck gently, a gesture that she found strangely intimate. It was all so new, even if it had been going on for more than two years now; so precious – so unlikely, too, but it had happened.

She sat down beside him. They were early – the concert was

not due to start until half past seven, forty minutes away. In the background, in the green room that gave directly off the bar, they heard one of the singers warming up.

'Listen to this,' he said. 'There's a bit here about a performance of *Lohengrin*. Leo Slezak, the Czech tenor, was due to climb on to a swan and sail off the stage. Unfortunately one of the stagehands sent the mechanical swan off before he had time to get on to it. So Slezak turned to the audience and sang, in German, "When does the next swan leave?"'

They both burst out laughing. 'I can understand the view that Wagner's inherently ridiculous,' Isabel said. 'Even when the swans run on time.'

Jamie nodded. 'But there are plenty of operas that one can't really take seriously. I've always had difficulty with *Pagliacci*. Everybody seems to die. I know it's tragic, but somehow one would have thought that at least one or two of the principal singers would be left standing.'

He slipped the magazine into the small music case he had with him and turned to Isabel. 'I'm sorry about the other night. I wasn't—'

She interrupted him. 'I'm the one who should say sorry. I dragged you there.'

'It's not that I dislike dinner parties,' Jamie continued. 'It's just that the people at that one . . .' He shrugged. 'The chemistry wasn't there. You know how sometimes things just zip along. I didn't feel it.'

'I know,' said Isabel. 'I could tell.' He had obviously not enjoyed himself, which had slightly surprised her, since she thought everybody else had.

He smiled. 'Anyway, let's not talk about it. This concert . . .' He trailed off.

Isabel knew there were occasions when Jamie did not look forward to a performance, and the shrug that he gave revealed that this was one.

'What is wrong with it? It looks interesting enough.'

He drew an imaginary line on the table, a casual, invisible doodle that she assumed divided the evening's offering into two. 'Some of the pieces are interesting. The others . . . well . . .' He reached for the programme that Isabel had bought in the lobby. 'Here. This new piece, "Melisma for the Return of Persephone". It's rubbish. I just don't like it. This is only the second time it's been played, which surprises me. Once would have been enough. Or too much.'

Isabel was surprised by this comment. Musicians could back-bite, but Jamie, she thought, was not like that; he was usually gentle. Something had irritated him profoundly for him to say this. 'Somebody must like it,' she said mildly. 'It must have some merit, otherwise . . .'

Jamie shook his head. 'You've got a touching faith in the way these things work, Isabel,' he said. 'Merit doesn't come into it.'

He was in an odd mood, she decided. 'All right,' she said. 'But don't let it worry you. And I'll try not to catch your eye during the performance.'

He had glanced at his watch, and she decided that it would be better to leave him by himself. She rose to her feet, explaining that she was going to go to her seat in the hall, where she would read the programme notes. He said yes, that was a good idea; he would see her afterwards and they would go back to the house together. Had she brought her car? She had, and had parked it conveniently behind the hall, outside the small, secondhand bookshop that specialised in science fiction. A bassoon was not an easy instrument to carry, and on the occasions when Jamie played the contrabassoon, difficulties of transport could become acute. The contrabassoon had eighteen feet of wood and metal tubing, and required a case that was almost six feet in length. Some contrabassoonists, Jamie had pointed out, were considerably smaller than their instruments – though this was not the case with him.

'Maybe they're compensating for being so small,' he had once suggested. 'A tiny tuba player must feel much bigger than he really is.'

Isabel thought this was possible; she had noticed small men in immense cars and sometimes there did appear to be a connection. Yet one had to be careful with observations of this type; it was very easy to be uncharitable, and then to regret it, as she had been and done once, when on holiday in Spain with John Liamor and they had been talking about ostentatious cars and inadequate drivers. They had been sitting in a pavement café, and at that moment an immense Mercedes-Benz had entered the plaza and had drawn to a halt near them. And Isabel had said: 'Yes, now look at him. He's making up for something.' John Liamor had said, 'Yes, obviously.'

Then the driver had got out of the car and raised himself with difficulty on to his two artificial legs.

The piece that aroused Jamie's disdain came immediately before the interval. Before the concert began, Isabel had the opportunity to read the programme notes and the composer's biography. 'Although not yet thirty, the American composer Nick Smart has attracted considerable attention for his bold and original compositions for both voice and chamber ensemble. In "Melisma for the Return of Persephone", this talented young composer, currently spending a year as composer-in-residence

31

at the University of Edinburgh, applies a technique of Gregorian chant to explore the vowels of Persephone's name. Mr Smart will be conducting his piece this evening.'

Isabel smiled to herself. Jamie did not like pretentiousness; and that, she thought, was why he had taken against 'Melisma'. She could understand that: the greatest beauty, she felt, was to be found in simplicity. Ornamentation had its place, but that place was a small one. And what, she wondered, had Persephone to do with it? It was unfortunate that Hades had seized Persephone and taken her into the underworld; Demeter was rightly distracted, as anyone would be in the circumstances, but . . . The concert was about to begin. She snatched a last glance at the small photograph of Nick Smart printed alongside his biography. A young man smiling at the camera, captured against a background of a college building, it seemed, somewhere old, in the new way that buildings are old in the United States, and . . . She peered at the photograph; the lights were dimming in the hall. Yes, he looked remarkably like Jamie. It was uncanny.

There were four short pieces before 'Melisma' began. Jamie played in the first two, and then slipped back on to the stage shortly before the outgoing conductor welcomed Nick Smart on to the podium. Isabel watched as a lithe figure, clad in the crumpled black linen suit habitually favoured by composers, ascended the steps at the front and shook hands with the man who now passed him his baton. So that was Nick Smart; although Isabel was in the third row from the front and therefore able to see the stage quite well, it was difficult to make out very much about the composer from behind. But even then, she thought that had Nick Smart been sitting at the bassoon rather than Jamie, she would not have known the difference.

'Melisma' began. Isabel closed her eyes and tried to follow the direction of the music, but it soon defeated her. The possibility of resolution was raised from time to time, but then quickly dashed as an unexpected chord intruded. Miasma, thought Isabel, this is a miasma. 'Miasma for the Confusion of Persephone'. Jamie would appreciate that, she thought.

She looked in Jamie's direction. It seemed that there was little for the contrabassoon to do in the early stages of the piece, but, towards the end, when the prospect of Persephone's release drew closer, there were rumbling bassoon sounds on the lower notes of the register, signifying, Isabel imagined, the depths of Hades from which the unfortunate girl would shortly be released. She suppressed a smile. Hell was more likely to be a place of white noise, the noise favoured by torturers, than a place of contrabassoon pedal notes. Or would Hell be an endless loop of boy bands, or rap? Either would be torture.

Of course, the abolition of Hell meant that such thoughts were now the merest fantasy. Isabel was agnostic as to what, if anything, lay in store for us after this life; that there was a world of spirit seemed to her to be a possibility that we should not exclude. Consciousness was an elusive entity about which we knew very little, other than that it came into existence when certain conditions were present – a sufficient mass of brain cells operating in a particular way. But could we really say much more than that about where it was located and whether it could survive in other conditions? The fact that a plant grew in one place did not mean that it could not grow in another. And if something lay behind this consciousness, orchestrated it and the conditions that produced it, then why should we not call this something God?

She closed her eyes. The key in which the music was now being played suggested that Persephone was out of the under-world and that flowers and grain were returning. She opened them. A few energetic bars more and the music suddenly came to an abrupt, unresolved end. No resolution. That is so *counter-intuitive*, thought Isabel. And if a composer does not resolve a piece then the applause should be similarly incomplete. One hand would be aimed at the other, but would stop short of actual contact: unresolved clapping.

Yet the applause was enthusiastic – thunderously so. Isabel looked about her at the faces of her fellow concert-goers; many were smiling enthusiastically. Of course, one had to be careful about reading too much into that; people could smile with relief at the end of an unsatisfactory piece, and even applause could be provoked by sheer joy at being released from some-thing one does not like. But this audience, she thought, meant it.

She did not go into the bar at the interval, since she knew that Jamie liked to socialise with his fellow musicians, and she would leave him to do that. So she went the other way, out to the front, and stood outside the hall for a few minutes, enjoy-ing the evening air. Others were doing the same, and she recognised some of them. There was a man she saw in Cat's delicatessen from time to time; there was a couple with their emaciated, earnest-looking teenagers; there was the young woman who worked in the fund-raising office of the univer-sity; and a few others. Isabel listened. Everybody, it seemed, was talking about 'Melisma for the Return of Persephone'. 'Really remarkable,' said the man from the delicatessen to the woman standing at his side. 'I've heard something by him before. He's going places, I think.'

'Yes,' said the woman. 'Very . . .' She left the word hanging.

Very unfinished, thought Isabel.

The woman finished her sentence. 'Very beautiful.'

Oh, really! thought Isabel.

The verdict from others was much the same. Oh well, thought Isabel. Perhaps I'm not sufficiently used to the language he's using. Music is not an international language, she thought, no matter how frequently that claim is made; some words of that language may be the same, but not all, and one needs to know the rules to understand what is being said. Perhaps I just don't understand the conventions by which Nick Smart is communicating with his audience.

She returned to her seat. The second half of the concert was very straightforward. Mozart's Flute Concerto in G and some German Dances from Schubert. At the end of the programme, she waited for a few minutes in her seat until the rush subsided, then made her way through to the bar at the back. She saw Jamie standing at the far end, his back to her, talking to a man and a woman. She went over to join him, negotiating her way through the press of people around the bar.

She reached out and touched him on the shoulder. 'I see what you mean,' she whispered, 'about poor Persephone. Ghastly . . .'

Nick Smart turned round and stared at her.

In her state of shock, it took a few moments for Isabel to work out what had happened. Jamie was there, but standing opposite the composer, whom she had taken for him.

Isabel thought quickly. 'Ghastly fate,' she said hurriedly. 'And poor Demeter: what parent could fail to sympathise with her!'

'I'm sorry,' said Nick Smart. 'I thought at first that you didn't like it.'

Isabel laughed. She looked desperately at Jamie, who was smirking. 'Heavens no. I thought it very arresting. Remarkable.' The man outside had used that adjective and she reached for it now.

'Yes,' said Jamie, coming to her rescue. 'Remarkable.' He paused. 'Nick, this is Isabel.'

Nick Smart took Isabel's hand and shook it. She thought: Anybody could have made that mistake. He looks very like Jamie; so much so, they could be brothers.

The young woman, whom Isabel recognised as one of the violinists and who had been standing next to Jamie, looked at her watch and muttered, 'Sorry. Must go. Glasgow train.'

Jamie said, 'Fine. I'll see you next time, whenever that is. Next month, I think.'

Isabel, her poise now recovered, turned to Nick Smart. 'I see that you're composer-in-residence at the university, Mr Smart. Do you have to teach?'

Nick Smart turned to her, but only briefly. When he replied, it was as if he were uttering an aside. 'A bit. Not much.' He turned back to face Jamie. Isabel noticed that as he did so, he smiled. American teeth, she thought, knocked into shape by expensive orthodontics but slightly worrying in their regularity.

'So do you play a lot for Scottish Opera?' asked Nick.

'Yes,' said Jamie. 'I stand in. Quite a lot.'

'I've been working on an opera,' said Nick. 'On and off.'

'What's it about?' asked Isabel.

It was possible, she thought, that Nick did not hear her question; either that, or he ignored it.

'The difficulty with a full-length opera is that there's just so much music,' said Nick, addressing Jamie. 'It's pretty difficult.'

'So I gather,' said Jamie.

Isabel looked to see if Jamie had noticed her question being ignored, but he did not. She glanced at Nick Smart, at the black linen suit. She noticed an expensive watch on his left wrist and a discreet signet ring. There was an air of expensive grooming about him. But there was something else, and she could not quite fathom it. Smugness? Narcissism? One thing was clear: he was not the slightest bit interested in talking to her; that had been apparent right at the beginning.

'Jamie,' she began. 'It's getting a bit late. I think . . .'

Nick moved his head slightly to glance at her; no more than that. Then he turned back to look at Jamie. A smile played about the edge of his mouth, a look of enquiry.

Jamie muttered something and took Isabel aside. 'Would you mind?' he asked. 'Nick has asked me to have a drink with him. Would you mind if I stayed?'

She thought: I do mind. I mind a great deal. But she said, 'No, that's all right. Will you be in later?'

He leaned forward and kissed her on the brow. 'Of course.'

Nick Smart was watching, bemused. His eyes moved away. He touched his watch with his right hand, a delicate gesture, as a conservator might remove dust from a painting with a silk cloth.

4

At breakfast the next day she said to Jamie, 'You changed your tune.' She had not intended it to sound like an accusation, but that is how it came out.

He had been feeding mashed-up boiled egg to Charlie, and he kept at his task as he replied. 'Why do you say that? What tune?'

'A metaphorical one,' she said. 'Nick Smart's piece, "Melisma for Persephone" or whatever it was called. You were . . . well, you were hardly enthusiastic before the concert. Then . . .'

He buttered a small piece of bread and spread white of egg across it. Charlie, watching eagerly, reached out to snatch the morsel. 'Gently does it,' said Jamie. 'There. How about that? Delicious, isn't it?' This is what babies are, thought Jamie: graspings and softness, splatterings of food, dribbles of liquid, small unintelligible sounds of creaturehood. He half-turned to Isabel, licking a small smear of egg from his fingers. 'I found it better second time round,' he said. 'Some pieces are like that. You hear things you've missed.' He paused and wiped his hand on a small piece of paper towel. 'Actually, one should always be prepared to listen to music again. I remember that when I first heard Pärt I missed a lot of the subtlety. I thought it was Philip Glass all over again. But it isn't.'

Isabel reached for a slice of toast and began to butter it. Charlie watched intently.

'And what was he like? Nick Smart? Were you impressed?'

Jamie reached forward and tickled Charlie under the chin. 'Very interesting. We had a good talk. We went to a bar down near the Pleasance. He has a flat over there, behind Surgeons' Hall somewhere. This bar was a real down-to-earth place. Locals standing there looking at you with that look . . . that appraising stare that you get when you go into a local pub where you don't belong.'

Isabel kept her voice even. I might have wanted to come, she thought. Had it occurred to him that she might have wanted to go along with them? 'And you talked music?'

'Mostly. He's quite an accomplished composer, you know. He was at Tanglewood last year, that place in New England, doing a summer seminar. They don't invite just anybody.'

'I'm impressed.'

If there was sarcasm, intended or otherwise, in Isabel's tone, then Jamie did not pick it up. 'Yes,' he said. 'He is impressive. And he suggested that we could work together on something. He's interested in writing something for the bassoon and wants to try some ideas out on me.'

She absorbed this disclosure in silence. Of course it was perfectly reasonable that Jamie should work with other musicians and composers; of course he had to do that. But for some reason, she did not like the idea of his working with Nick Smart. She wanted Nick Smart to go away, to not be there.

She swallowed. 'Good,' she said. 'It sounds as if you'll enjoy that.'

He's without guile, she thought, and his reply had that note of boyish enthusiasm that so appealed to her. 'Yes. I'm really excited about it. I love working with composers. And he's the real thing, Isabel.' He picked up Charlie's plate and scraped at the last vestiges of boiled egg. 'But I can't work out why he should want to work with me. Why me?'

Isabel looked at him, and looked away again sharply. She had an idea, but she would not spell it out for him. Not yet.

Jamie had the entire morning and part of the afternoon off. He had cut back on his teaching commitments recently in order to give himself more time for rehearsals and the occasional recording sessions that he had begun to do. This meant that he was also more available for Charlie, which of course Isabel encouraged, although Grace did not. Grace regarded herself as being responsible for Charlie during the day, in order to give Isabel time to devote herself to her work. Or that was how she dressed up her desire to keep Charlie to herself as much as possible. Fathers are all very well for when they're older, she told herself, but when they're small, as Charlie still is, they need women to look after them. Jamie picked up Grace's unspoken jealousy, but sailed through it regardless.

That morning he would take Charlie to the museum, he decided. They could have something to eat in the cafeteria and Charlie could be shown some of the working models of machinery, held up against the glass cases so that he could see the intricate whirring models within. He had watched these with some interest on the last occasion that Jamie had taken him there, although it was not clear whether he had the remotest idea of what was going on. A bassoon could equally well be a steam engine, and a steam engine a bassoon, thought

40

Jamie, reflecting on the fact that for Charlie the world was probably just shapes and sounds.

Isabel had once remarked to Jamie that it would be interesting to know what would happen if a mysterious virus were to wipe out everybody older than four, leaving the world to infants and toddlers. Presumably all these small children would be like Charlie, faced with the models of machines, uncertain what everything was.

'Would we learn what everything was for?' she asked. 'Or would we have to invent things all over again?'

'It would be one great feat of reverse engineering,' said Jamie.

Isabel was not so sure. 'What about music notation?' she asked. 'Would we eventually work out what musical scores meant, if we had nothing to base our knowledge on?'

Jamie thought we would, although he doubted whether anybody but the four-year-olds would stand a chance. 'Those aged one, two and three would pretty quickly fall by the wayside,' he said. 'Because the four-year-olds, who might just be able to fend for themselves, would not do anything for the younger ones. Four is too young for altruism.'

She thought about this. Would it really be as William Golding had predicted in *Lord of the Flies*? The thesis behind that was that children left to their own devices reverted to savagery, but it was really just a mirror image of the savagery of the adult world; remove the adults and the children fell into tribalism and superstition. But if the resulting childish dystopia merely reflected the adult world, then what happened if one removed the adults – in other words, the authority figures – from the adult world? What if we really did kill God, what then? Would we all be rationally committed to the greater

41

good, or would savagery be the norm? To kill God: the idea was absurd. If God existed, then he should be above being killed, by definition. But if he was just something in which we believed, or hoped, perhaps, killing him may be an act of cruelty that would rebound upon us; like telling small children that fairies were impossible, that Jack never had a beanstalk; or telling a teenager that love was an illusion, a chemical response to a chemical situation. There were things, she thought, which were probably true, but which we simply should not always acknowledge as true; novels, for example – always false, elaborately constructed deceptions, but we believed them to be true while we were reading them; we had to, as otherwise there was no point. One would read, and all the time as one read, one would say, mentally, *He didn't really.*

But now Isabel had other things to think of. Charlie was going off with Jamie; Grace was tackling a large load of washing, somewhat grumpily, but tackling it none the less; and she had agreed to meet somebody for a cup of coffee at Cat's delicatessen.

'Who are you seeing?' Jamie asked when she told him that she had the appointment. 'Somebody about the *Review*?'

'No,' said Isabel. 'It's somebody we met at that dinner the other night. She was sitting on the same side of the table as you were. That woman who was there by herself. Stella Moncrieff.'

Jamie seemed largely uninterested. None of the guests had made an impression on him that evening, and he was unsure as to whom Isabel was talking about. 'Oh yes.' He stood up to lift Charlie out of his high chair.

'Yes,' said Isabel.

He turned away from her, holding Charlie to him. Tiny fingers were grasping at his hand; there was sweet, milky breath on his cheek, soft breath like that of a small animal. Words had such power, greater power, even, than music, and it still hurt him to hear Cat's name; hurt him and filled him with a disconcerting feeling of excitement. Cat. It was a name redolent of desire, of sex – Cat. It still had that effect, when he knew that it should not, when he willed that it should become like any other name, stripped of its power to rekindle feelings that he did not want rekindled.

As she walked along Merchiston Crescent, Isabel thought about what Jamie had said about Nick Smart. She should not become possessive; she knew that. It was the worst thing that she could possibly do, as it would be massively resented by Jamie if he were to detect it. If she was to keep Jamie, then she should not suffocate him; he had to have his freedom, had to have his own life, and that life included time spent with other musicians. I-Thou, she thought, remembering Martin Buber; the Thou has a part to it that I cannot possess. She could not expect to like all of Jamie's friends, nor could he be expected to like all of hers. She did not care for Nick Smart, but that was because Nick Smart, she decided, had not liked her; that had been obvious on their first meeting. But why should he take against her? Her apparent faux pas over 'Melisma' had been defused through her quick explanation, so that could not be the reason; there was something else. Because I am a woman, she thought; that was it. Because Nick Smart does not like women and, in particular, he did not like women who had claims on the man with whom he was engaged in conversation. I am not the jealous one here, she thought; there was an entirely other sort of jealousy operating.

She put Nick Smart out of her mind and thought about the

telephone call that she had received from Stella Moncrieff. She had not masked her surprise at the call, and the other woman had evidently picked this up. 'Yes, I know that this is unexpected,' she said. 'But I had hoped to have the chance to speak to you privately the other night. Somehow the occasion didn't arise. I hope you don't mind my getting in touch with you now.'

'Of course not. And I'm sorry we didn't have the chance to talk.'

She had been on the point of inviting Stella to the house but had stopped herself and suggested instead that they meet for a cup of coffee at Cat's delicatessen. This would give her the ability to bring the meeting to an end when she wanted to; it was difficult to do so when the other person was a guest in one's house; short of lying about having to go out, of course.

Now, as she stood before Cat's window and stared admiringly at the imaginatively arranged display of foodstuffs, she found herself looking forward to the meeting with Stella Moncrieff. There was something to be discussed, she thought, and the most likely topic, surely, was the other woman's husband and what had happened to him. Isabel's curiosity had been aroused by what had been said to her at the dinner, and now, she thought, she would get a further explanation as to why he should be ashamed to show himself in public. The modern world was a tolerant place: even murderers brazened it out these days; they wrote their memoirs, telling all, and publishers fell upon them with delight. There was no shame there, she thought, unless the memoirs included an apology to the victims, which they usually did not; on the contrary, they sometimes blamed the victims, or the police, or their mothers, or even, in the case of one set of memoirs, the mothers of the

44

police. Mothers, of course, were to blame for a great deal; Vienna had established that beyond all doubt. But that was another matter; the immediate question was that if shame had been so convincingly rendered old-fashioned, de trop, then why should anybody feel unable to attend a dinner party on the simple grounds that he stood accused of doing some nameless thing? And what could that have been? Some sexual peccadillo, no doubt, that made him seem ridiculous; some sad story of middle-aged loss of self-control, a momentary aberration, a little thing, probably, but enough to drive him into shamed retreat. The press, in particular, was cruel, rushing to cast the first stone, luxuriating in the humiliation of its victims.

She went inside. Although two of the four coffee tables in the corner were vacant, there were quite a few other customers examining or ordering food from the counter. Cat, who was serving cheese to a tall, rather angular woman, looked up when Isabel came in and smiled a greeting. Isabel smiled back; the days of open warfare in her relationship with Cat were over now, or so she hoped. Even if she seemed slightly remote from him, Cat had accepted the existence of Charlie and had for-given Isabel for having him with Jamie, her former boyfriend. Nor did Cat resent Jamie's presence in her aunt's life, although Isabel was careful to avoid situations where she was together with Jamie in Cat's presence, just to be on the safe side.

Isabel decided that Cat would be too busy over the next little while for them to talk, and so she made her way directly to one of the vacant tables and sat down. There were always interest-ing overseas newspapers in Cat's delicatessen, often *Corriere della Sera*, but sometimes examples that were more recondite, for Scotland at least: the *Straits Times*, the *Globe and Mail*, *The Age*, several days old, perhaps, but none the less interesting for that.

Today she found a copy of the *Washington Post* dated four days previously, and she began to page through it, skipping over the news of electoral campaigns that seemed to go on and on for ever. There was a review of a new opera at the Kennedy Center, together with a picture of the composer and librettist at the premiere, alongside various society figures. The society figures dressed as expected, one of the women sporting a tiara and all the men having that air of slick grooming and benevolence that accompanies real wealth. Rich people, thought Isabel, never looked anxious in photographs; they looked relaxed, assured, untouchable by the worries of lesser mortals.

'Isabel?'

She looked up. Eddie, Cat's timid assistant in the delicatessen, the damaged boy who had been taken on and nurtured, was standing before her, wiping his hands on the floury apron he was wearing. More progress, thought Isabel; there had been a time when Eddie had been unwilling to don the apron on the unexpressed grounds that it was unmasculine; or those were the grounds that Cat and Isabel had inferred. Now he felt sufficiently sure of himself to wear it, and Isabel felt pleased. Little by little, whatever trauma it was that Eddie had experienced – and she had a good idea of its nature – was receding in the face of his increased confidence.

'Nice apron,' she said.

The words came out automatically, but it occurred to her just as automatically that she should not have said anything.

Eddie hesitated. He looked down at the apron and then looked up again. He smiled.

'It's really for lassies.'

Isabel shook a finger at him playfully. 'No, Eddie. We don't say that sort of thing any more. Men do women's work, or what

46

used to be women's work, and vice versa. It's the same with clothes.'

Eddie looked at her disbelievingly. 'You mean that men wear women's clothes? Dresses?'

Isabel shrugged. 'Some do,' she began, and then laughed. 'No, I didn't mean that. I meant to say that the categories of what's for men and what's for women have blurred. We share so much now.'

Eddie decided that the conversation had gone far enough. 'Are you going to have coffee?' he asked. 'Cat said I wasn't to keep you waiting.'

Isabel explained that she was expecting to be joined by somebody, but that he could bring her a coffee anyway if he did not mind coming back for a second order once her guest arrived. Eddie nodded.

'And what are you up to these days, Eddie?' she asked.

'The usual.' He paused. 'Well, the usual, and something else. I'm taking a course.'

Isabel expressed her pleasure. She had hoped that Eddie would eventually get round to obtaining some sort of qualification. He was intelligent enough, she thought; once again it all came down to confidence. She enquired what the course was. He had once mentioned a catering certificate that one could start by post and then go on to finish at catering college. Was it that?

'Hypnotism,' announced Eddie.

Isabel stared at him. 'Hypnotism?'

'Yes. I've been doing it for six weeks now. There's one lecture a week, Thursday nights, at college. You don't get an actual certificate, but you do get a bit of paper at the end saying that you're licensed to hypnotise people.'

Isabel thought this unlikely. 'A licence? Surely not.'

Her disbelief took Eddie aback, and he started to become defensive. 'It's not the sort of hypnotism you see at those shows,' he said. 'We don't make people eat an onion and think that they're eating an apple. We don't make them see things that aren't there.'

'I'm glad to hear it,' said Isabel. 'I should hate to find myself eating a raw onion at your behest, Eddie.'

'It's about hypnotising people to help them stop smoking or . . . or doing other things that they don't want to. Bad habits. Hypnotism can cure bad habits.'

'I'm sure it can,' said Isabel.

'And past lives,' Eddie went on. 'You can take people back to their past lives.'

Isabel thought: We're in Grace's territory now. Had Eddie been put up to this by Grace? 'Are you sure?' She looked at him enquiringly and he inclined his head. He was perfectly serious.

'My friend Phil is in the class too,' said Eddie. 'He allowed one of the girls – I forget her name – to regress him. I was there. I watched it. It was at Phil's place after the class. We'd gone back there and Phil asked to be regressed.'

Intrigued in spite of herself, Isabel asked what Phil had been in his previous life. 'A coal miner,' said Eddie. 'A coal miner up in Fife. Somewhere near Lochgelly.'

That, thought Isabel, is progress. There were too many exotic previous incarnations; too many Egyptian princesses, too many figures of minor royalty, too many Napoleons, no doubt. A coal miner from Fife had the ring of authenticity about it.

'And then,' Eddie continued, 'she took Phil one life further back.'

'And what was he then?' asked Isabel.

'Robert the Bruce,' said Eddie. 'I'm not making this up, Isabel. I swear. He was Robert the Bruce. Phil was. He didn't open his eyes or anything. He just said "I'm Robert the Bruce" when we asked him who he was.'

'Fancy that!' said Isabel. 'Phil, of all people! Robert the Bruce.'

'Aye,' said Eddie. 'It was dead spooky, Isabel. He started talking about a battle and how he was going to defeat the English.'

Isabel opened her mouth to say something, but the door opened and Stella Moncrieff walked in. She looked across the room, searching for Isabel, and Isabel gave her a wave.

'My friend,' Isabel said to Eddie. 'Could we carry on our conversation some other time?'

Eddie nodded. 'Any time, Isabel. And I'll regress you too, if you like.'

'All right,' said Isabel. 'But you do realise, don't you, that I'm likely to be Bonnie Prince Charlie? Or possibly Louis the Fourteenth?'

Eddie looked at her with the air of one about to disabuse another of a fondly held notion. 'No you won't,' he said. 'Women are women in their previous lives and men are men. You'll just be a woman, Isabel. Same as you are now.'

Stella Moncrieff began with an apology. 'I haven't kept you waiting too long, I hope.'

Isabel indicated the chair on the other side of the table. 'No, you haven't. I arrived just a few minutes ago.'

Isabel glanced at Stella as she sat down. She was one of those people it was difficult to place in age terms, but Isabel thought that she was probably somewhere in her early fifties. The trouble, of course, was that clothing no longer provided a cue; middle-aged clothing still existed, but the middle-aged no longer wore it; jeans had liberated them from all that. So now the only way of distinguishing between those who were twenty and those who were forty was by the age of the fabric of the jeans: threadbare cloth meant twenty, cloth integral meant forty, the reversal of what one might expect. Until you looked at the face, of course, or, more tellingly, directly beneath it, at the neck, and then you could tell. That's where the years showed, like rings in the trunks of trees. And no trick of the surgeon could deal with that; Isabel wondered why people bothered with plastic surgery, with the nips and tucks, the stretching and plastering that left the victim looking like the mask of a Japanese Noh actor, flattened, pinned back in perpetual discomfort. Who was that unfortunate queen, she asked herself – an earlier queen of the Netherlands, was it not – who was one of the first to have plastic surgery and had been left with a perpetual smile? And then her husband had died and the surgeons had been obliged to perform frantic corrective surgery so that the queen should not appear to be too cheerful about her husband's death.

Isabel smiled at the thought, and Stella Moncrieff returned the smile.

'It's good of you to see me,' she said. 'I sat at the telephone for ages, plucking up the courage to call you.'

The frankness of this remark struck Isabel. 'But why? Why worry about phoning me? I'm not . . .' She trailed off. None of us is.

'Oh, you know how it is. You meet somebody briefly, and you wonder whether they want to hear from you.'

'I was delighted to hear from you. I hoped that we might

have had a longer conversation the other evening. But dinner parties of that size . . .'

Stella nodded. 'You know, I had asked them to invite you . . . I wanted to meet you, you see.'

Well, thought Isabel, that at least explained the invitation; it was nothing to do with Jamie. She hesitated for a moment, and then decided to be as frank with Stella as Stella was being with her. There was something about the moment which prompted confession. 'Well, I was wrong about that,' she mused. 'I thought that they had invited me because of Jamie.'

Stella looked blank.

'The young man I was with,' Isabel said.

For a moment Stella's puzzlement continued. 'The young man with . . . with the dark hair? That lovely looking one?'

Isabel felt an intense flush of pleasure. He was lovely looking. It was not just a case of her looking upon him with a lover's eyes; lovers will make anything lovely. 'Well, yes,' she said. 'I suppose he is.'

There was still something Stella did not seem to understand. 'You were with him?'

Isabel's pleasure began to turn into annoyance. 'Yes,' she said. 'We have a child together.'

The disclosure unnerved Stella, who struggled to maintain her composure. 'Of course . . . But, why would they have invited you because of him?'

'To see him. To inspect him. It's fairly recent. And, well, people have talked about it a bit. He's a few years younger than I am.'

'I could tell that.' It slipped out, and could not be retracted. But Isabel did not care. She had decided that she liked Stella.

'Anyway, from what you tell me it had nothing to do with Jamie.'

51

'No. It was me. I wanted to meet you, you see. And I'm afraid I seem to have very little confidence these days. I know it's silly, but it's just the way things are.'

Isabel decided to take the initiative. 'I heard something,' she said. 'That doctor I was sitting next to, the cardiologist, he said that there had been some issue with your husband.'

Stella looked away. 'That's one way of putting it.' She paused and looked back up at Isabel. 'The truth of the matter, Isabel, is that I want you to help him. I know that you don't know me. I know that our troubles have got nothing to do with you, but that's the problem, you see, our troubles have got nothing to do with anybody. Except us.' She made a gesture of despair. 'So what am I to do? I can't do anything myself, and Marcus, that's my husband . . . he's paralysed with guilt and self-reproach. With shame, too. He'll hardly leave the house. Won't talk to his old friends.'

Isabel listened carefully. It was not clear to her why Stella had chosen her. She decided to ask.

'Because I've heard about you,' said Stella. 'I knew somebody you helped a couple of years ago. Nobody asked you. You just helped. And you made a difference.'

Isabel noticed that Eddie was signalling from the counter, making a gesture towards the coffee machine. She nodded to him and then said to Stella, 'They make a particularly good cappuccino here. Would you . . .'

'Yes. Please.'

'And then you can tell me exactly what the problem is. I can't imagine that I'll be of any use, but tell me anyway, and I'll do what I can.'

It sounded so trite to her, even as she said it; the stock scene from the detective novel. The investigator reassures the distraught wife. Find out who's blackmailing/having an affair with/holding prisoner my husband, please. Don't worry, I'll do what I can. And then the relief on the face of the supplicant.

Stella looked relieved.

Isabel stopped herself short. Don't make light of human pain, she told herself. It's not funny.

5

That evening, on impulse, Isabel said to Jamie, 'Look, it's five o'clock, or just about. If we bathed Charlie now and gave him his—'

'Tea,' supplied Jamie, pointedly, but smiling as he said it. He wanted to use the popular Scottish word for what Isabel would have called dinner, or possibly supper.

'If you like,' said Isabel. 'I was going to say dinner, as you well know. But then, if you're going to be all down and demotic, dinner means lunch in such circles, doesn't it?'

'Feed,' suggested Jamie. 'How about that as a compromise?'

Isabel did not think so. 'Give him his *feed*? It sounds like agriculture to me. You give feed to cattle, don't you? Anyway, after he's had his—'

'Grub.'

'All right, after he's had his grub, why don't we . . .' She paused. 'Grub first, then ethics. You know who said that?' It was an accurate description, perhaps, of the daily routine of the editor of the *Review of Applied Ethics*, which did indeed begin with breakfast and proceed to ethics.

Jamie did not hesitate. '*Erst kommt das Fressen, dann kommt die Moral.* Brecht.'

Isabel bowed her head in mock homage. 'I'm impressed.'

'My German teacher at school went on about that,' said Jamie. 'He said that *Fressen* was appropriate for animals rather than people. Brecht was showing his low opinion of humanity by choosing to say *Fressen* rather than *Essen*. That's why grub is a better translation than food. Grub is messy, animal stuff. He was very clever.'

'He was a hypocrite,' said Isabel. 'He lived very comfortably in the GDR. No belching Trabbi for him. And he supported those horrific people who ran the place.'

Jamie shrugged. 'He believed in communism, didn't he?'

'Yes,' said Isabel. 'But he enjoyed what other writers in the GDR were denied. Freedom.' It was tawdry, that shabby republic, with its legions of informers and its unremitting greyness, its rotten, crumbling concrete. And then it had all gone so quickly, as in a puff of smoke; the whole Soviet empire, with its deadening tentacles of fear, collapsed and discredited, vanished like a confidence trickster who has been exposed. And yet there had been so many who had connived in it, had derided its opponents; what had they to say now? Her thoughts turned to Professor Lettuce, who had been a founder of something called the East-West Philosophical Engagement Committee. He had gone to East Berlin, as had Dove, and had publicly complained about reactionaries, as he described them, who had questioned the visit on the grounds that meetings would be restricted to those with posts in the universities, Party men every one of them. Dove ... She thought of his paper on the Trolley Problem; she felt a vague unease about that, and she felt that there would be more to come.

55

But Brecht and the GDR, and even Dove and Lettuce, seemed far away. 'Let's leave Brecht out of it for a moment,' she said. 'After Charlie has been *fed*, I thought we could go out to the Pentlands and just . . . just go for a walk. Up past the reservoir. Charlie could go in the sling. He's getting a bit heavy for that, but you can carry him. He'll probably just nod straight off. It's such a lovely evening.' And I want to talk to you, she thought. I want to be with you.

They drove out on to the Biggar Road, leaving the last of the town behind them. Isabel was at the wheel of her green Swedish car and Jamie sat in the back, to keep Charlie company in his car seat. At Flotterstone, a few miles round the back of the Pentland Hills, they turned off the main road and parked in the small car park set aside for hikers. Then, Charlie safely installed in the sling affixed to Jamie, they set off up the winding road into the hills. Jamie gave Charlie a finger, and the child gripped it tightly. 'Look,' said Jamie, nodding in the direction of the little fist around his index finger. 'Look.'

Isabel smiled at the sight. She had watched the process of Jamie's falling in love with Charlie, watched every step, from the first surprise and discovery to this emblematic moment, each act of tenderness by Jamie confirming the diagnosis of deepening love. Nothing had been said, and she thought that it was right that this should be so; the declaration of love could weaken its mystery, reduce it to the mundane. To say on the telephone, love you, as she heard people doing, was dangerous, or so Isabel thought, because it made the extraordinary ordinary, and possibly meaningless. Good day meant nothing now because it had become an empty formula; *love you* could go the same way. It was significant that it had already been shortened, and the I had been dropped. What did that mean? That people were too busy to say I love you, or too embarrassed by the subjectivity of the full expression?

They began their walk, following the narrow road that worked its way up between the fold of the hills. The road, which was not used by ordinary traffic, was bordered on either side by an undulating stone dyke. To their left, all the way down to the bed of a small river, the throaty gurgling of whose waters could just be heard, was a slope on which Scots pines grew, their branches host to crows, which cawed and flew away. On the other side of the road, beyond the lichen-covered stones of the dyke, fields swept up the hillside; fields interrupted here and there by clumps of gorse, in flower at this time of year, the dark green foliage spiked with small clusters of yellow. Blackface sheep, hardy enough for the Scottish hills, dotted the fields, paused in their grazing and stared vacantly at Isabel and Jamie as they walked past, then dropped their heads again, unconcerned, and moved away.

'Charlie's asleep,' whispered Jamie. 'Off like a top.'

She peeked at him. 'It must be the most wonderful feeling, being carried like this. Warm and secure. Why would one want to grow up?'

Jamie laughed. 'Why indeed?'

They walked on. They were now drawing level with the reservoir which covered the flooded floor of the glen. The road they were following traced a route round the side of it before making its way up to the head of the glen, to peter out at the just-visible buildings of an isolated sheep farm. The surface of the loch was still, as there was no wind, no breeze, and the sky ahead, high and empty, was reflected on the water; no clouds, just blue. She turned to Jamie and took his hand, easily, unself-consciously. The touch of him thrilled her, and she shivered.

'I met Stella Moncrieff for coffee this morning,' she said. 'Remember, I said I was going to do that.'

He was looking up, trying to make out something halfway up the hill. 'And?'

'Well, she wanted to see me. She's asked me to help her with something.'

As Isabel expected, this caught Jamie's attention. He turned to her. 'Isabel . . .' There was an unmistakable note of warning in his voice. Jamie did not approve of Isabel's getting involved in matters that did not concern her and had told her as much, on numerous occasions.

'Yes,' she said. 'Yes.' And then, after a few moments, 'I could hardly refuse.'

Jamie shook his head. 'But that's exactly what you could do,' he said. 'Life consists of refusing things we shouldn't be doing.'

Isabel reflected on this for a moment. Perhaps for some people life did indeed consist of refusing to do things – there were those who were adept at that. But she was not one of them. Her problem, rather, was one of deciding which claims on her moral attention to respond to and which to ignore; and it seemed, for some reason, that there were always more of the former than the latter. How can we ignore a cry for help? she asked herself. By steeling our hearts? By closing them?

She stopped and turned to Jamie, placing a hand on his fore-arm. Behind him, above the hill, a bird of prey circled watchfully; the evening sun, still with a touch of summer warmth in it, touched the heather with gold. At this time of year in Scotland it would be light until eleven at night; further north, in the Shetlands, it would never get dark at all. At midnight the *simmer din* would make it possible to read a newspaper outside without strain to the eyes.

'Don't you want to know what she asked me to do?' He could hardly say no, she thought.

He sighed. 'All right.' They began to walk again, and he added, 'But I don't approve. You know that, don't you?'

She held his arm lightly, and began to tell him about her conversation with Stella. Marcus, Stella's husband, was a doctor.

'What sort?' asked Jamie. 'Everybody's a doctor in Edinburgh. Or a lawyer.'

'An infectious diseases specialist – a very highly regarded one, apparently. Or he used to be highly regarded.' She went on to explain what Stella had told her. Marcus, she said, had been at the forefront of work on MRSA, the so-called Super Bug, which had been the cause of a growing number of deaths in hospitals.

'Apparently quite a few people are carriers of this,' said Isabel. 'You or I might quite innocently have it. In our noses, I'm sorry to say. Our systems keep it under control, but we can pass it on to others, who can't cope with it.'

Jamie looked down at Charlie, at his tiny nose. 'And?'

'And he was doing a trial on a new antibiotic,' Isabel continued. 'One that can knock this MRSA on the head. A drug company has come up with a pretty good candidate and has been given a licence to produce it in this country. Marcus had been involved in the clinical trials and was monitoring its use in patients.

'Everything was going perfectly well, and then, very much to his surprise, a patient who had taken the drug developed pretty serious side effects. Heart palpitations, Stella said. And another one turned up with the same sort of thing. Alarm bells started to ring.'

If Jamie had been indifferent to the story at the beginning, he no longer was. 'What was that drug that was so disastrous? The one that people used before they realised that it caused terrible birth defects?'

'Thalidomide. I suppose this was a bit different. The patients were all right, even if things were a bit scary for them. Anyway, Marcus was asked by the health authorities to look into these cases. He did that, and he also published a report in a medical journal in which he showed that both of these patients had been given a massive overdose of the drug: one was a drug addict and had self-administered it in the deluded belief that he would get some sort of hit from it; the other was the victim of a nursing error. So he claimed that everything was fine and that the drug was perfectly safe within the limits they set for this sort of thing.'

She sensed Jamie's absorption in the story, and was pleased. 'But,' Isabel went on, 'there was an unpleasant surprise around the corner. A few weeks later he published his findings, in the form of a letter in one of the big medical journals, and a few weeks after he had said everything was perfectly safe, a man up in Perthshire was given the drug and promptly died. There was an enquiry and the hospital authorities took a closer look at Marcus's original report – the one that said that everything was perfectly all right. And what did they find?'

Jamie frowned. 'That he'd made a mistake?'

'Yes. But more than that. The data in his original paper was shown to have been falsified. It was something to do with the level of the dosage.'

They walked on. Jamie was lost in thought; then he spoke. 'I see where this is going. The implication was that he had an interest in keeping the drug manufacturers happy and that he falsified the figures for their sake. For money.'

That was not what Stella had suggested, Isabel explained. She had said that although the press had had a field day and blamed Marcus for the death, they had not accused him of doing it for money. But he had been reported to the General Medical Council and he had been heavily censured for issuing a misleading report. He resigned from his university chair too and stopped all medical work.

'A rather sad story,' said Jamie. 'Sad for everybody.' He paused. 'And she wants you to . . .' He looked at Isabel. 'She wants you to clear her husband's name? Is that it?'

Isabel nodded.

'Oh, Isabel!' exclaimed Jamie. 'What's this got to do with you? What's this got to do with being the editor of the *Review of Applied Ethics*, for heaven's sake?'

'Everything,' said Isabel.

Jamie looked puzzled. 'I'm sorry . . . ?'

'She says that he's completely innocent. That's what it's got to do with me. An innocent man is now consumed with shame for something he didn't do. That has something to do with all of us, I would have thought. And it just so happens that I have been asked by his wife to do something about it. That brings me into a relationship of—'

'Moral proximity with him,' said Jamie. 'Yes, I know all about that. You've told me about moral proximity.'

'Well, then,' said Isabel. 'There you have it.'

'But how can you believe her – just like that?'

'She seemed to me to be telling the truth.'

'But what wife wouldn't? Of course spouses protest that their spouses are innocent. Mothers do it too. Presumably Mrs Stalin took the view that her son Joe was widely misjudged. That he would never have run a terror.'

Isabel laughed. 'One cannot expect objectivity from a spouse, I suppose. But then I have somebody else's view to go on as well. That cardiologist I sat next to at the dinner told me that he was convinced that Marcus was innocent. He didn't tell me at the time what it was that he was supposed to have done, but he did tell me that he thought he didn't do it. That's two views in favour of innocence.'

They had reached the end of the reservoir, and Jamie now glanced at his watch. 'We should go back now,' he said. 'We'll need to settle him.' He planted a kiss on the top of Charlie's head, on the tiny tam-o'-shanter he was wearing. Then, when they had started to retrace their steps, he said to Isabel, 'I'm sorry I sounded so discouraging. You want to do this, don't you?'

'Yes,' said Isabel. 'I do.'

'Then I'm proud of you,' said Jamie. 'Really proud.'

And with that he leaned over towards her and kissed her. She touched his hair. She breathed in. I am so in love, she thought, so deeply in love; and love of one is love of another, and another, until all humanity is embraced and the heavenly city realised, which will never happen, not even in your lifetime, Charlie, she thought.

With Charlie put to bed, Jamie said, 'I'll cook.'

It was now almost nine in the evening and Isabel had not thought much about supper. She had a vague idea that they might have a plate of the moussaka that she had made the previous day and which needed to be finished off, but she had done nothing about it and Jamie's offer was particularly welcome. He would make pasta, he said; he had discovered some porcini mushrooms in the larder and some cream. 'Not very adventurous,' he said.

'Delicious,' said Isabel. 'And thank you. I want to look at some things in my study.'

She left him in the kitchen and went through to her study at the front of the house. She had a fax machine there, and there was often a small pile of papers disgorged from it at the end of the day, waiting for her attention: scribbled notes from the printers, queries from the copy editor, and, in this case, a report from a reader. That was what she had hoped for, and she caught her breath when she saw it.

She had sent Dove's paper on the Trolley Problem to two referees, as was normal with any unsolicited paper. She had been scrupulously careful in her choice of referee; it would have been easy to pick a harsh one – and she knew at least one professor of philosophy, himself seldom published, who delighted in finding fault with the work of others and recommending against publication. Isabel would not use him as a referee, although when Professor Lettuce had been in charge of the board he had taken to doing so off his own bat. This man, whom Isabel had nicknamed the Harsh Critic, was friendly with Lettuce. Two peas from the same pod, thought Isabel; Lettuce seemed to attract vegetable metaphors, she admitted – the great turnip. No, she would not send it to the Harsh Critic because he would reject it more or less automatically – or would he? If he, the Harsh Critic, was friendly with Lettuce, then might it not be possible that he would be on good terms with Lettuce's acolyte, Dove, the oleaginous one? In which case he would probably recommend in favour of publication, as he would not like to cause Lettuce to wilt. This made matters more complex. If she decided against the Harsh Critic, then she was taking away from Dove a chance that he would otherwise have, and she wanted to treat him with scrupulous fairness. But no, he would get a random referee, one chosen by her when she opened her address book at random . . . like this, and there he was, the obvious choice, her friend Iain Torrance. Iain, a theologian with a philosophical background, was as fair-minded a man as one could meet, and, what was more, he had a reputation for working quickly, as he had done now. Lying on the floor, having slid off the desk on which the fax machine was placed, was his faxed report – a neatly typed page subscribed at the bottom with his signature: *Iain*.

She reached down to pick it up. Her hand, she noticed, was shaking. She perched on the arm of one of her library chairs; the seat itself was stacked with papers, the chair having long since ceased to be anything but part of her filing system. There were three paragraphs; two lengthy ones and a final, short one. She skimmed through the first two and then came to the third. It could not have been clearer.

'I much regret,' wrote Iain, 'that I find no original insights in this paper. The arguments advanced by previous participants in the discussion are repeated, but not developed. And that part of the paper which purports to be a further refinement of the original conditions of the bystander's plight do not add anything. Try as I might, I cannot think of any respect in which this paper helps a problem which already has a certain hoariness to it. Paper and ink are finite. I cannot recommend they be squandered on this article.'

She put down the report and closed her eyes briefly, as if to order her thoughts. She left her study and went back into the kitchen. The pasta was simmering on the stove, misting up the windows, but there was no sign of Jamie. Then she heard the piano, and smiled. They sometimes sang together, or he sang for her; now she heard him.

He stopped as she came into the morning room. He laid his

hands gently on the keyboard, at rest, and smiled at her. She wanted to run to him, to hug him to her, this young man who had come to her so unexpectedly, who brought music, a child, beauty, all these things into her life. But she contained herself, and asked, 'What was that again? It was so haunting.' It was.

'"The Parting Glass",' he said. 'It's one of those songs that has a complicated history. There are Irish versions and Scottish versions. Burns joined in and did a version too.'

'Of course. I've heard it before. Could I hear it again?'

'Here,' he said. 'Take this glass of wine. And hold it. That's how you should listen to it. Take a sip.'

She took the glass of white wine from him. It was still chilled, with tiny drops on the outside. She moved it in her hand, feeling the cool of it, the wetness.

Jamie said, 'This song makes me feel sad.'

She watched him.

He began to sing, and the words, which he enunciated so carefully, and the slow movement of the melody, touched at her heart:

Oh, all the comrades that ere I had
Are sorry for my going away
And all the sweethearts that ere I had
Would wish me one more day to stay
But since it falls unto my lot
That I should rise and you should not
I'll gently rise and I'll softly call
Good night and joy be with you all.

He finished and gently closed the lid of the piano. She did not move.

'Why did you sing that?' she asked.

Jamie looked up. 'Sometimes I just feel that way,' he said. 'I feel sad when I'm happy. It's strange, isn't it?'

She thought of the words: *But since it falls unto my lot / That I should rise and you should not* – words of leave-taking, every bit as moving as those used by Burns in 'Auld Lang Syne', and with perhaps an even greater poignancy to them. Why, she wondered, did we need loss and parting to remind us of how much friendship, and indeed love, meant to us? Yet we did.

6

She did not tell Jamie that she was going to see Marcus Moncrieff the next morning. It was true that he had accepted her involvement, but she suspected that his acceptance was a reluctant one and that he would not really want any further details. Perhaps he had come to the realisation that this is what she did: she became involved, and he had simply decided that he might as well let her get on with it. She wondered whether it was the same as accepting that one's partner smoked, or drank rather too enthusiastically, or read frivolous novels; bad habits all, but ones with which one might just have to live. She found herself using the word partner against her will; it insinuated itself into her thoughts; linguistic resistance was difficult, and ultimately futile: there was no point in continuing to call Beijing by its long-established anglophone homonym when a whole generation had forgotten that it was once Peking.

She thought that it was a good sign that Jamie was becoming more tolerant of her involvement in the affairs of others; it showed, she thought, that he accepted her for what she was. Isabel had been perfectly self-assured in all areas of her life until that fateful night when she and Jamie had made the transition from friends to lovers. We can be confident in our dealings with the world when what the world sees is the outer person, with all the outer person's defences: the intimacy of a love affair is a different matter altogether. And who might not feel just the slightest bit insecure under the gaze of a lover – a gaze which falls on birthmarks, on blemishes physical and psychological, on our imperfections and impatience, on our human vulnerability? And how more so when one is older and the lover is younger.

Jamie made everything different, and she was blessed by his presence. But by accepting him into her life she had given a hostage to fortune: he could become bored with her; he could leave her; he could suddenly find her ridiculous. None of which she thought would necessarily happen, but it could. So this sign that he approved of her was important. Yet I am not to think about this, she reminded herself.

Peter Stevenson, her friend whose advice she sought on all sorts of matters, had been explicit. 'Isabel, you must stop fussing about this!' he had said, his voice revealing his irritation. 'You and Jamie are together. The age gap is a little unusual. But so long as you are both happy, which you are, it doesn't matter. And Charlie's arrival has created a bond between you which will last for the rest of your lives. So stop fussing, for heaven's sake.'

The three of them, Peter, his wife Susie and Isabel had been walking along the Water of Leith together, having had lunch in the Dean Gallery, when Isabel had said something about not wanting to crowd Jamie. The Stevensons had asked them to dinner at West Grange House and she had been hesitant in her acceptance.

'I'd love to come,' she said. 'Yes, of course.'

'And Jamie too,' said Susie. 'We meant both of you. Charlie will settle, won't he?'

'I'll bring Charlie,' she said. 'I'm not sure about Jamie.'

'But you can choose the evening,' said Susie quickly. 'We'll fit in around you.'

Again Isabel had hesitated. 'It's not that,' she said. 'It's just that . . .'

Peter had looked at her quizzically. 'Doesn't Jamie want to come?'

They had reached the point where the road dips down to the Dean Village at the old millpond and the path along the river begins. High above them were the soaring stone arches of the Dean Bridge, at the end of which a private house, built into the rock, acted as the bridge's anchor to the wall of the valley. It was one of Edinburgh's astonishing architectural details; a house which had been lived in for many years by a prominent psychiatrist, who used to joke that since the Dean Bridge had traditionally been the bridge of choice for suicide, like the Golden Gate in San Francisco, his house should have borne a sign reading Last Psychiatrist Before the Dean Bridge. Some had frowned at this, but Isabel had appreciated the joke; doctors needed their moments of dark humour amidst all the human suffering of their day. She looked up. How long would it take to fall – should the psychiatrist's counsel prove ineffective – and what would one think on the way down? The Roman Catholic Church used to be charitable in such matters and had been prepared to concede that people probably changed their minds on the way down from these great heights, that the desire to die became a desire to live once the descent began. Repentance, then, could be assumed, and in this way one went up rather than down, in the metaphorical sense; once, that is, one had come down. Did the Vatican still think this, she wondered, or was it no longer necessary to make scholastic distinctions of this nature, if Hell had been abolished in Catholic teaching, as it had by liberal Protestantism? She had never been able to understand how anybody could reconcile the existence of Hell with that of a merciful creator; he simply would not have embarked on us in the first place in order to send us to some Hieronymus Bosch-like torture chamber or its more modern equivalent (a place of constant piped music, perhaps). Hell might be an airport, she thought, lit with neon and insincere smiles. No, she told herself; she was prepared to accept the possible existence of a creator, in the same way as she was prepared to accept curved space, but he or she would not invent Hell, whatever twists and turns on the subject of free will and choice were resorted to by the concept's apologists. Why would a creator want us to have free choice in the first place if we were bound, imperfect creatures that we are, to abuse it? And yet, she thought, who amongst us does not want there to be justice, does not relish the idea that when Stalin took his final breath what he was shortly to encounter was at least some measure of punishment for his countless murders, rather than forgiveness? We should be careful, she decided, about abolishing Hell, even if we have no proof of its existence; and yet, and yet . . . Was not it a part of growing up to under-stand that much as we may yearn for a universe ruled by perfect justice, this was not the way the world would ever be? The wicked got away with their wickedness more often than not, and became incorrigible as a result: the robber barons became richer; the swaggering bullies never met anybody stronger than themselves. The most that many could hope for was that justice took the occasional victory, and that they would see it and be comforted.

She looked away from the bridge. It made her dizzy to look up, even more so than looking down. I could never live up in the air, she thought, like people who inhabit high apartments, with nothing below them but an almighty drop and eagles for company.

Peter's question needed to be answered. 'I'm sure that he'd like to come,' she said. 'It's just that—'

There was an edge to Peter's interruption. 'It's just that *what*, Isabel?'

It was not easy to explain. She was sure she was right in thinking that Jamie would not want to feel *taken over*; what young man would? 'It's a little difficult,' she began. 'I don't want him to think that he has to tag along with me.' Even as she spoke, she knew that it sounded unconvincing, and the way in which Peter and Susie were looking at her confirmed this: Peter was frowning, in an effort to see what exactly Isabel was driving at; Susie looked sympathetic, but it was evident that she did not agree. And that was when Peter told her to stop thinking about the age difference.

For a while she was silent. They had continued on their walk, leaving the bridge behind them. The river, which was in full spate, was louder now, and she had to raise her voice to be heard above the sound of the water.

'Easier said than done,' she said.

Peter thought about this. 'All right,' he said. 'Advice is always easy to give. But that doesn't make it any less relevant.' He looked at her quizzically. 'Don't you realise that Jamie probably feels about you exactly as you feel about him? Hasn't it occurred to you that he can probably hardly believe his luck – to have found an attractive, intelligent – I could go on – witty woman like you? What would his alternatives be? Any other woman I can think of would be boring by comparison with you, Isabel. So stop it. Right? Just stop it. Subject closed.' He drew breath. 'Except for one final thing. You're, what are you, forty-something? Forty-three? That's still young . . . ish. And it's not all that much older than him. Fourteen, fifteen years? So what?'

'So does that mean we're all to come to dinner?' Isabel asked. All three laughed.

'Yes,' said Peter. 'It does.'

They continued with their walk. Then, as they drew level with St Bernard's Well, with its small stone temple to Hygena, she saw a figure ahead of them. He had been walking towards them and now he suddenly turned and walked the other way, back towards Stockbridge. She had not been paying attention; there were a few people on the path and he was just one of them. But then she realised who it was. Nick Smart.

She stared after the retreating figure; he was a swift walker. Peter noticed.

'Seen a friend?' he asked.

'No,' said Isabel.

They stopped to admire the temple. Isabel glanced down the path; Nick Smart must have let himself into Moray's Pleasure Gardens, as he had disappeared from sight. She felt vaguely puzzled. Did he live there, in Moray Place or Doune Terrace? The gardens were private, and one needed to be a key-holder to get into them. And had Jamie not said something about his living over in the Pleasance somewhere, quite a different part of town.

'People used to come and take the waters here,' said Peter. 'Apparently the water tasted foul. Full of iron.'

'But that would have been a plus,' said Susie. 'Smelly mineral water was always thought to be better for you. More potent.'

Isabel remembered visiting a spa in France where the water was traced with arsenic, and much sought-after for that reason. We like our pills bitter, she thought.

Peter had remembered something. 'We visited Vichy once,' he said. 'I remember that it was at the end of the season and there was an orchestral concert in the public gardens. The mayor made a speech at the concert and concluded by saying that he hoped to see all the *curistes* back again next year. Which I thought was rather tactless.'

Isabel asked why, and Peter explained. 'Because presumably they hoped to be better,' he said. 'And if they were better, they wouldn't need another cure the following year.'

Isabel felt foolish. 'I see. Of course.'

Peter looked at his watch and suggested that they walk back to the gallery, where they had left the car. As she walked, Isabel wondered about Nick Smart. Why had he turned round so suddenly? Had he seen her coming? And if he had, then why should he wish to avoid her?

Stella Moncrieff had said: 'He said that he'll see you. At first he said no. He was adamant – you know how stubborn men can be. But we can be stubborn too, can't we? And I insisted. I begged him. I said that he should see you if only for my sake. And eventually he said that he would.'

Isabel did not particularly like the idea of anybody being forced to see her; the position, she thought, that dentists must find themselves in when a young and nervous patient is led to the chair. Dentists, of course, could console themselves with the fact that the encounter was in the patient's best interests, whereas she was not so certain that her seeing Marcus Moncrieff would do him any good. She had agreed to the meeting because Stella had pleaded with her and because she felt that it was her duty to respond, but that did not mean that her heart was in it. In fact, right up to the moment that she left the house at eleven o'clock that morning she had hoped that Stella would call and say that the whole thing was off. But she had not, and Isabel had set off on foot for the Moncrieff flat in Ramsay Garden.

The city was preparing for the annual arts festival, which was now only a few weeks away. During that time, for a spell of just under a month, it would become another town altogether – a great open amphitheatre of plays and concerts and opera. Jamie would be busy, both as a player and as a spectator, and they had paged through the programme together, selecting what they wanted to see. Even Charlie had a programme outlined for him: a concert of performing dogs, to be held in a tent, and a magic show described in the programme as being 'completely suitable for those under two'. 'But everything's magic for them,' Isabel had said. 'Have you noticed how he laughs if you hide your fingers under the tablecloth? He thinks that's terribly clever.'

For the inhabitants of Ramsay Garden, the Festival brought only the promise of sleepless nights. Their proximity to the Castle Esplanade, on which the military tattoo was performed each evening during the Festival, meant that they had to endure massed pipe bands every night, along with all the pyrotechnics, the fireworks and explosions, that the military, and large sections of an enthusiastic public, consider to be artistic. The final movement of the 1812 Overture, with its cannon fire, was a gift for such an occasion, and was being performed that year, adding to the assault on the senses of those who lived nearby. At least, thought Isabel, as she glanced up at the immense structure which had been erected on the esplanade, at least the modern inhabitants know that the bangs and explosions were not real; earlier inhabitants of that spot would have quaked at such sounds, which would have meant real cannon fire. And the skirl of pipes would have heralded the arrival of troops, and trouble.

She reached the Moncrieffs' door. A small brass plate said, simply, Moncrieff; along the edge of the plate was etched a tiny art nouveau device, one of those curious vines that artists of the period liked so much. The inhabitants of Ramsay Garden were playing the game, keeping in period, just as the inhabitants of the Georgian New Town on the other side of Princes Street were doing their best to maintain a Georgian style. The city encourages actors, thought Isabel, as probably all iconic cities do; look at the Parisians; it must be such an effort being so Parisian. She smiled at the thought, and pressed the bell. She herself lived in a Victorian house, but was not sure how she should respond to that particular challenge. By being stern and disapproving? By clothing the legs of pianos to preserve modesty? *If* the Victorians had ever really done that, and she had her doubts. Mind you, had there not been a Victorian librarian who had insisted on keeping books by men and women on separate shelves – unless, of course, the authors were married, in which case the books might properly be placed side by side?

Stella greeted her and gestured for her to come inside. She looked relieved, Isabel decided; as if she had worried that I would not come.

'I'm not late, I hope,' Isabel said. She knew that she was not, but it was something to say.

'Of course not. You're . . . well, you've come exactly when I expected you.'

Isabel looked about her. They were standing in a generously sized entrance hall. Off to the right, which was the back of the building, there was a door that led into a kitchen, and a short corridor off to further rooms, the bedrooms, she imagined. Then, to the front, another door, attractively panelled in light oak, opened out into a room which, although Isabel could not see into it, she assumed would be the drawing room. That was the room which looked north, which would have the famous Ramsay Garden view, and there was light flooding in from it.

She glanced at the furniture, at the walls. It was typical of an Edinburgh flat of a well-heeled professional couple, which she assumed was what the Moncrieffs were – or had been; this was a house that had seen social disaster, she reminded herself.

'Marcus is through there,' said Stella, gesturing to the drawing room. Her voice was lowered; the hushed tone one might use outside a hospital room.

She led Isabel into the room. At first, after the comparative gloom of the entrance hall, the light seemed overwhelming. It suffused the room, flooded it, and made Isabel blink.

'Facing north,' she said, 'and yet this is so bright.'

Stella muttered something about the windows, but Isabel did not catch what she said. Her attention was now focused on a man sitting in a chair by the large expanse of window at the front. He turned his head as they entered and rose to his feet.

'Marcus,' said Stella, her voice raised slightly, as if she were talking to a child. 'Isabel Dalhousie has arrived.'

As Marcus rose to greet her, he was dark against the glow behind him, a chiaroscuro effect that created what felt, Isabel thought, like an annunciation scene. She moved towards him, towards the light, and they shook hands.

'The view . . .' said Isabel.

They both turned to look out. 'Yes, that's a view, isn't it?' said Marcus. 'I sit here and see something different virtually every moment.' He gestured towards Fife, where the hills, dark green and solid, were sharply outlined against the sky, like sections of a collage. 'The sky over there changes constantly. Constantly. It shifts from blue to white to purple just like that. It's very bright right now for some reason.'

But Isabel was gazing downwards, to where the flanks of the Castle Rock descended almost vertically to the douce order of Princes Street Gardens, the railway line, the floral clock, the benches. Her gaze drifted beyond that, over the tops of the buildings, the crude, grey architectural mistake of the New Club, the ridges of chimneys, the stately stone pediments, to Trinity in the distance, and then the silver band of the Forth. The heart of a country, she thought; the heart of this place.

There was a chair opposite his, and Marcus invited her to sit down. As she did so, she cast a quick appraising eye over him. He was a man somewhere in his fifties – the younger end, she thought – tall, just beginning to grey, and with one of those slightly angular faces that spoke of intelligent determination. It was a face which would have looked good on a banker, or a senior lawyer, but would do well for a doctor; a trustworthy face. And not at all aggressive, she thought. This was the face of a kind man.

His voice was soft, the words clearly articulated, each syllable given its value, and each r given more. It was what she would have described as an old-fashioned Scottish professional voice.

Of course he was innocent, that cardiologist was right – she could not imagine his doing anything underhand.

'You know, I'm not sure whether Stella should have bothered you with my troubles,' he said. 'This wasn't my idea, you know. This meeting of ours. Not my idea.'

'I'm only here because I want to be,' said Isabel. 'I assure you.'

He smiled, a quick, wistful smile. 'That's good to know. I'm not sure whether I'm here because I want to be. I rather think I'm not.'

Here in what sense? Isabel wondered. At this meeting with her, or here in this room, rather than elsewhere – at work, in a hospital or clinic? And there was a final possibility: here on this earth.

'When your wife . . . when Stella spoke to me, I doubted if there was anything I could do to help you. I told her that. But if there is anything . . . well, it's sometimes useful to have somebody else go over things and see if there is anything that can be done.'

He watched her as she spoke, a slight smile playing about his lips. 'It's very kind of you,' he said. 'I wouldn't want you to think me ungrateful, but frankly I don't really see any way out of my . . . misfortune. It's happened. That's it.'

Isabel felt his sense of defeat. There were times when the acceptance of defeat must seem the only option and an intelligent person in such circumstances might well become resigned.

'Would you be able to tell me – very briefly – what happened to you?'

He sighed. 'Very well. I was a doctor. I still am, I suppose. Although, as you can see, I'm not actually practising any more. I'm an infectious diseases specialist.' He had been looking at his hands as he spoke; now he raised his eyes to meet hers. 'There

78

was a time when everybody thought that they wouldn't need us much longer. People thought that they'd won the battle against the microbe – but were we in for a little surprise on that front! Everything has come back with a vengeance. TB is the least of it, perhaps. The real nasties, Ebola, Marburg and the rest, are lurking, and of course all sorts of new ones – avian flu and so on.'

Isabel nodded. 'I suppose we've created exactly the right conditions for this,' she said. 'Too many people. Too much travel. Environmental degradation.'

Her comment seemed to cheer him: she knew what she was talking about. 'Exactly,' he said, his voice becoming enthusiastic. 'Global warming is going to wreak havoc with health. Malaria in Europe and North America. And that will be just the beginning.'

She brought the conversation back to his case. 'But I was told that you were working on MRSA when this . . . this thing happened.'

His enthusiasm visibly waned. 'I was. I was very interested in a new antibiotic that had just been licensed. I knew the people who made it – one of the smaller drug companies, a bit of an outsider. They had a veterinary preparation and an anti-fungal cream, and then this very clever bit of chemistry. It was like finding oil for them.

'Anyway, any cases of MRSA infection in Scotland were more or less referred to me and I monitored the use of this drug. Everything was fine. Then, by highly unlikely coincidence, two cases turned up in Edinburgh, one after the other, of patients who had taken the drug experiencing fairly serious side effects. Heart issues. I was asked by the Scottish government health people to look into it. The chief medical officer was concerned.

'I did it. I got hold of the records and had blood samples sent back for analysis. I tried to find out what happened.' He paused. 'Are you following me?'

Isabel smiled. 'So far. You've been very clear.'

He ignored the compliment, turning to stare out of the window. 'We looked at the two patients. There was an interesting thing about one of them. He was a drug addict. He had got hold of our antibiotic from some pusher who said that it was a new drug that would give an unusual hit. How the pusher got his hands on it is beyond me, but it was probably theft from a pharmacy somewhere. These people will steal anything, sell anything, and take anything. As long as it's a pill. And then word gets out on the street that something works and you have all sorts of people overdosing on the most peculiar substances. Laxatives even. Vitamins.

'I spoke to this patient and asked him how much he had taken. He gave me an answer which worried me, as it was not all that much in terms of an overdose. Ten times the therapeutic dose, in fact, but that will be well within the limits of tolerance of that particular drug. Those limits are pretty large.'

He looked back at Isabel. 'I don't know if you've had any dealings with addicts. Have you? Do you know what they're like?'

Isabel thought. There had been a student in her college at Cambridge who stayed in bed all day and made no sense most of the time. There had been a person in the apartment next to hers when she had been on that fellowship in Georgetown. He was an addict, she had been told, but he appeared perfectly inoffensive. A bit thin, perhaps, but inoffensive. I have had a sheltered life, she thought.

'No. I can't claim vast experience.'

'Well, I'll tell you something about them,' said Marcus. 'Everything they say has to be distrusted. Everything. And so although I was worried, I thought that the chances were that he was lying. So I got hold of the blood that had been taken from him when he was admitted and sent it off to the lab for re-analysis. And when it came back, the result showed an over-dose of about one hundred and fifty times the therapeutic dose. So this patient had swallowed a whole carton of the drug. But then that's what they do. When they're desperate, they pump the stuff in with reckless abandon.'

Isabel wondered what happened to the patient. She could not see him in her mind's eye, for some reason. He was just a story.

'He recovered,' said Marcus. 'He was discharged and went back to wherever he came from. Fife, I think. He's probably overdosed on something else since then. Poor man. He won't be long for this world, I suspect. But no sooner had we sorted him out than another one turned up. In this case the patient had been given a dose of the drug by a nurse here in Edinburgh. The nurse swore blind that the dose had been the normal one, but again the blood showed a massive overdose. Not as big as in the addict's case, but pretty massive. Nobody could work out how on earth it happened, as the patient sided with the nurse and confirmed her story.'

'So somebody was lying?'

He thought for a moment. 'Not necessarily. Errors can be made in how things are written down. Inadvertently move a decimal point one place in either direction and you get very different results, don't you? But something had gone spectacularly wrong. Again, we were able to sort things out and the patient recovered reasonably well. She was a nice young woman, actually. A student at one of the universities, as I recall.'

'So you wrote up these results?'

'Yes. I made a report to the chief medical officer. I effectively gave the drug a clean bill of health. Then I wrote the two cases up as a case note for one of the medical journals. They published it. It was just a couple of paragraphs describing what had happened.'

'Then?'

Marcus was silent for a while. Isabel noticed that his hands, clasped together in his lap, were white at the knuckles. His voice, when he spoke again, sounded strained.

'A month later a man in Glasgow was admitted to hospital. He had been treated with the antibiotic. He . . . I'm sorry to say that he died from heart complications. He had not received an overdose – that was established. The press got hold of the case and they asked how somebody could die from taking a licensed medicine. Well, I could have given them an answer to that, but they were not in the slightest bit interested in a rational explanation about inevitable risk. They put pressure on the minister and they took another look at my report. They discovered that the doses I had described did not match a new set of lab reports on the blood. The figures were way out. And they also discovered that I had not declared a conflict of interest when I published that case note. I should have told them that I had received a research grant from the company that made the drug. And they were right: I should have done that. I don't know why I didn't. It was some years ago. It must have slipped my mind.

'There was an internal enquiry and I was censured. They said that I had been negligent in not checking the blood results when they were so obviously exceptionally high. They said that a prudent doctor would have had the samples tested again. They censured me too for not disclosing the conflict of interest and the journal published a withdrawal of my case note.'

He stopped and looked at Isabel. The air of defeat had returned. He seemed flattened, almost as if the breath had been knocked out of him – winded.

Isabel felt that she needed to think. She rose to her feet and stood before the window, looking out over Princes Street below. A train had emerged from the tunnel underneath the National Gallery and was moving slowly west. She looked at her watch. That was the Glasgow train, which left every fifteen minutes.

'So what they did,' she said, 'is to conclude that you were negligent. Is that it? They didn't conclude that you had deliberately falsified anything?'

Her question seemed to unsettle him. He looked down at his hands for a few moments before he replied.

'There was no falsification,' he said. 'There was an error in the transcription of the results somewhere along the line. It's possible that it was a slip by a medical student who was attached to my unit at the time. They accepted that. They said, though, that I should have rechecked and should not have relied on a medical student. They said that I was careless. That was the actual word used: careless.'

'And do you think you were?' asked Isabel.

He closed his eyes. She noticed that his right eyelid was twitching. 'Yes. I should have checked. And I should have declared the conflict of interest. I failed to meet the standards expected of a doctor of my experience.'

There was something that Isabel was unsure about. Was this

failure directly linked with the Glasgow case? She asked him this, and again he took a little while to answer.

'According to the press it was,' he said. 'One or two of the papers went so far as to accuse me of . . .' He faltered. 'Of killing the patient in Glasgow. They said that if I had done my work properly, safeguards would have been put in place. The drug would not have been given to somebody with a history of heart problems – which that man had. They blamed me for his death.' The next words were chiselled out. 'Publicly. Unambiguously.'

Isabel reached out and put her hand on top of his clasped hands. 'But you weren't responsible for that,' she said. 'Somebody made a mistake. That's all.'

But there was something she still needed to know. Why had he not checked the results, if they were so out of line with what might have been expected?

His answer came quickly, and Isabel thought that it sounded rehearsed. But then she realised that repetition may have the same effect as rehearsal. He would have had to explain himself a hundred times before, sometimes, perhaps, even to himself; of course it would sound rehearsed. 'It didn't cross my mind,' he said. 'It didn't occur to me that the results could be wrong. I took them at face value.'

They spoke for a few more minutes. Isabel asked him the name of the assistant who had worked with him, and he gave it to her. But he added, 'It was definitely not his fault. It really wasn't.' Then Stella appeared, hovering anxiously about the door. Isabel said goodbye to Marcus, who had sunk back in his chair and started to stare out of the window again.

Glancing behind her, Isabel whispered to Stella. 'He looks very depressed,' she said. 'Has he seen a doctor?'

'He won't,' Stella replied. 'I've tried. I've tried everything.'

'All right,' said Isabel. 'Give me a week. Maybe ten days. Then telephone.'

Stella reached out and briefly held Isabel's arm. 'You're a saint,' she said.

The compliment surprised Isabel. She did not conceive of herself in those terms at all; it simply would never have occurred to her to do so. A saint with a young boyfriend, she thought. And a taste for New Zealand white wine. And a tendency to think uncharitable thoughts about people like Dove and Lettuce. That sort of saint.

7

'People don't realise,' Cat said. 'They don't realise what running your own business is like. It's always there. Day in, day out. And you can't get away when you like. You're tied down.'

'Like having a baby,' said Isabel.

She had not intended to make the comparison, but it had slipped out. And she acknowledged that even if this was true for most women who had babies, it was hardly true for her, with her resources, with Grace to support her. While tact required that one should not complain about those respects in which one is better off than others, it also required that one should not complain about things that others did not have at all – such as children. Isabel was unsure about how Cat felt about not having a child herself, although she had a boyfriend now – 'the one after the last' as Grace had called him.

The last had been an apprentice stonemason, although Isabel still thought of him as a bouncer, the job he had been doing before he started to work with stone. He had the physique of a bouncer, and the physiognomy too, including a protruding jaw that must have been a very tempting target for those whom he was called to expel from the noisy subterranean club on Lothian Road that employed him. Isabel had met him a couple of times and had suppressed the urge to stare at him in a way which would have revealed her astonishment that such a man should be the choice of her niece. As if Cat's choices said anything about Isabel – of course they did not, she told herself, but still . . .

In fact she knew exactly what it was that attracted Cat. It was the same thing that she had seen in Toby, her skiing wine-dealer boyfriend; that she had seen in the one who followed him, the one to whom Isabel had never been introduced but whom she had spotted Cat with, arm-in-arm, walking along George Street one Saturday; and that she had seen in Christopher Dove – Dove of all people! – when she had had that brief flirtation with him. Cat was attracted to tall, well-built men; it was as simple as that.

It may have been simple, but Isabel thought that it was also incomprehensible. She understood that everyone had their preferred physical type, but she found it odd that this could be the sole factor in somebody's choice. One may find the combination of dark hair and blue eyes, for example, a heart-stopping one, but would one want to spend time in the company of dark-haired, blue-eyed people who had nothing to say, or, if they did have something to say, it was trite or even distasteful? She thought not. The problem was that the search for beauty was something that we were destined to conduct, in spite of ourselves; we wanted to be in the presence of beauty because somehow we felt it rubbed off on us, enriched our lives, made us more attractive. This was felt even by those who themselves were attractive; beauty sought beauty. Cat was tall and attractive, and clearly wanted tall and attractive men; that the men she found were empty vessels had not deterred her at all. But none of them had lasted, thought Isabel, which showed that the consolations of beauty were not long-lasting: there had to be something else.

Cat was talking to her, and had said something that Isabel had not caught. Now she repeated it.

'I don't like to ask you,' said Cat. 'But you said that you really enjoyed looking after the delicatessen. The last time that you did it, you . . .'

'Yes,' said Isabel. 'I enjoyed it. And I don't mind doing it again. You have only to ask.'

They were talking in Cat's office at the back of the delicatessen, and now she sat back in her chair, relieved that Isabel was volunteering. She had wondered whether she dared leave Eddie in control, but had decided that she should not. It was not that he did not know enough to run the shop – he could handle any of the tasks involved in keeping the delicatessen going – but he lacked confidence. Cat had seen it before, on occasions when she had left him in charge for a few hours: everything would be all right when she came back, but Eddie would be anxious, his relief at her return quite palpable.

Cat explained that a friend had invited her to join her for ten days in Sri Lanka. She could fly from Glasgow to Dubai, she said, and then from there to Colombo. Helen, her friend, had a boyfriend who knew somebody who had a villa. They had taken the villa for a couple of weeks and a party of them was filling it up.

'Are you going by yourself?' Isabel asked.

Cat looked at her sideways. 'Yes. Just me.'

There was a brief silence. 'I wasn't prying,' said Isabel softly.

Cat hesitated. Then, 'You can pry if you like. I don't mind.

He's called Martin, but I'm afraid that he's not the one. We're still seeing each other, but I just don't know.'

'If your heart's not in it, what's the point?' said Isabel.

Cat shrugged. 'You're right. But then it's not all that easy breaking things off. Particularly if the other person is still keen.'

'Which he is?'

'Which he is.'

Cat was looking at her in a bemused way, and Isabel wondered whether she was expected to say anything more. But what could she say about this Martin, this man she had never even met, and about whom she knew nothing. She could assume, of course, that he was tall and well built, but beyond that she could only speculate. Martin: the name gave nothing away. At length she said, 'You probably don't want to hurt him, do you?' It was a trite remark, but it led to her adding, 'So don't string him along. Tell him it's over.'

It appeared to be what Cat had wanted. 'I will. I'll tell him before I go to Sri Lanka.'

Isabel winced. Her advice had been seized upon, and this made her uneasy. She knew her niece, and understood that if Cat came to regret her decision to end her relationship with Martin, then she would lay the blame at Isabel's door, even if subtly.

'It must be your decision, of course,' said Isabel. 'I wouldn't want to interfere.'

Again Cat looked at her in bemusement; her niece shared Jamie's view that she interfered too readily and far too frequently. But this time Isabel had told her what she wanted to hear – that the relationship with Martin should be brought to an end. The decision taken, she felt a strong sense of relief. She was free.

★

Cat left for Sri Lanka on a Sunday morning, and Isabel took over on that Monday, arriving at the delicatessen shortly before Eddie. Grace had come to the house early, pleased to be placed in sole charge of Charlie for the entire day. She had already mapped out his week: a journey on the bus to her cousin in Dalkeith; an outing to the café at the Chambers Street museum; several trips to the Botanical Gardens – 'He loves the squirrels,' she said. 'And the hot houses too.' Isabel knew from a friend's report that Grace pretended that Charlie was hers. This friend had been standing behind her in a café at the zoo and had complimented her on Charlie's Macpherson tartan rompers. Grace had replied that she was part Macpherson, as if that were the explanation for Charlie's attire. She had not said that Charlie was hers, but had certainly implied it, not knowing, of course, that it was a friend of Isabel's who was addressing her. Isabel had been saddened by the story; she could so easily have been in Grace's position, had Jamie not turned up; and had it been she who was taking somebody else's child to the zoo, she might well have wanted others to think the child was hers. Who amongst us was above such longing, such pretence?

Eddie came in and hung up his green windcheater on the back of the office door. He always wore the same thing, Isabel had noted: a pair of blue jeans, blue trainers with white laces, and a curious long-sleeved white tee-shirt. She had never seen him in anything different, although he obviously had several pairs of jeans and several tee-shirts, since his clothes were always clean.

'Will she be there by now?' asked Eddie, looking at his watch.

'Yes,' said Isabel.

Eddie looked thoughtful. 'Where is it?' he asked. 'I've heard of it, but I've never really known. Is it somewhere . . . somewhere near Egypt?'

Isabel's eyes widened in surprise. 'No,' she said. 'Not really. It's near India. It's the teardrop off India.'

'Oh,' said Eddie.

Isabel watched him. There were so many people who knew very little about the world, and Eddie's generation knew less than most. She wondered, in fact, what he did know. Would he know who David Hume was, or Immanuel Kant, or Aristotle?

'Aristotle,' she said, on impulse.

Eddie frowned. 'I don't know about that,' he said. 'I've never sold any myself. Has Cat ordered any?'

Isabel looked away and muttered something about checking on it. She had not intended to expose him, and she knew that she should not laugh. There were plenty of people who would not know who Aristotle was, but there were not many who would think that he was . . . a cheese.

She entered Cat's office and switched on the lights. Cat had left a list of things to be done, and Isabel now went through it. There were to be several important deliveries, including a large one of Parmesan cheese, two wheels of it. Could she cut that up, Cat asked, and vacuum pack it with the vacuum pack machine? Eddie knew how to operate that, Cat explained, although sometimes it made him anxious. She thought about this: why should anyone be anxious about a vacuum-pack machine? She remembered her psychiatrist friend, Richard Latcham, telling her that free-floating anxieties could settle on anything – anxiety, like love, needs an object, and that could be anything.

A tempting smell of freshly ground coffee reached Isabel

through the open door of the office. She put down Cat's list and joined Eddie at the counter. The coffee was for her.

'Do you eat breakfast, Eddie?' she asked, as she cradled in her hands the warm mug he had passed her.

Eddie shook his head. 'No. Never. I have a cup of coffee when I come in here and one of those biscotti things.'

She looked at him. He was wiry, flat-stomached; there was no spare flesh. Eddie was good-looking, she thought, in a very boyish way, with his close-cropped light brown hair and the freckles that dotted his cheeks. He could have been a Scottish version of a boy from a Norman Rockwell poster, Isabel thought; one of those boys who delivered newspapers from his bicycle or dispensed sodas in the drug store, open-faced Midwestern boys who belonged to an altogether more innocent era. There was an innocence about Eddie – a sense of being slightly surprised by the world. And the world had surprised him, she remembered – surprised him badly.

'You should eat breakfast, Eddie,' she found herself saying. 'You need it.'

The young man shrugged. 'I'm not hungry in the mornings.'

Isabel looked at him again. If he lost a few more pounds he would begin to look anorexic. But did young men suffer from anorexia, as young women did? She vaguely remembered reading somewhere that they did, although much less frequently. Perhaps that was changing as boys became more like girls.

It proved to be a busy morning, and when Isabel next looked at her watch it was almost one thirty. Things slackened off slightly then, and they each took a quick lunch break. Then in the early afternoon, a dishevelled man came in and stood in front of the counter, staring at the cheese. Eddie asked him if he could help him, but was brushed away. He looked to Isabel for assistance.

As Isabel approached the man he raised his eyes and met her gaze. 'I want some cheese,' he said. 'I want some cheese.'

Isabel smiled encouragingly.

'What sort?'

'That one,' he said, pointing to a large piece of gorgonzola.

Isabel peeled on a plastic glove and reached down to extract the gorgonzola.

'I haven't got any money,' said the man.

She paused. Her hand was just above the cheese. Eddie, standing behind her, nudged her gently.

She hesitated. The man had a cadaverous, hungry look about him, but it was not her job to feed him. This is a delicatessen, she thought; it is not a soup kitchen. But then, on impulse, she lowered her hand, took hold of the cheese, and lifted it out of the cabinet.

Eddie watched her as she began to wrap the cheese in greaseproof paper. He was glowering at her. 'Cat wouldn't . . .' he whispered. 'Cat . . .'

'Don't worry,' Isabel replied. 'I'll pay for it.'

'Don't bother to wrap it,' the man said suddenly. 'I want to start it now.'

She let the wrapping paper fall away. She had noticed that the man had the lilting accent of the Western Islands.

'Where are you from?' she said, as she handed the cheese over the counter.

'Skye,' he said. And then added, 'A long time ago.'

She smiled at him as he took the cheese, and watched as it stuck to his fingers, which were stained and dirty. He licked at his fingers, and then took a bite out of the cheese. She watched him, and thought of the place from which he had come, a place of mountains and green pastures, of a green sea coming in from the Atlantic, the edge of Scotland, the outer limits of a world. What had brought him here, from that place – a failed croft, a mothballed fishing boat, enlistment in the army? And now this penury and hunger in a prosperous city that had no place for him.

'It's better with biscuits,' said Isabel, reaching for a packet of water biscuits off the shelf behind her. 'Take these too.'

He took the biscuits and stuffed them into the pocket of his coat.

'Thank you,' he said, and turned to leave the shop.

Eddie glared at Isabel. 'Cat wouldn't like that,' he said.

Isabel remained cool. In the past she had hoped that Eddie would become more assertive, but she had not imagined that he would assert himself against her. 'Oh yes?'

'Yes,' said Eddie. 'You can't give food away to just anybody who comes in and asks for it. This is a shop, you know.'

Isabel raised an eyebrow. She wanted to say: this is my business, and nothing to do with you. But it was not in her to be abrupt to Eddie; not to this injured boy. 'How much should I put in the till?' she asked calmly. 'Five pounds?'

Eddie turned away. Isabel could sense his anger in his voice. 'I don't care. It's up to you.'

She quickly forgot about the cheese incident, but it appeared that Eddie did not. Halfway through the afternoon, Isabel suggested that he take a break; trade was light, and she could watch the counter. No, he said, he did not need a break.

'You're still cross with me?'

Silence.

She waited, but there was no response. 'Look, Eddie, I'm

sorry. I know it was wrong of me. You have to work here all the time and you obviously can't have people coming in and asking for free food.'

He glared at her. 'No.'

Isabel tried to explain. At least he had said something, even if it was only no. And sometimes the word no is all that one will get, as at the famous occasion on which Proust and James Joyce had been brought together, and all that Proust had said was *non*. 'I shouldn't have done what I did,' she said. 'I acted on impulse. You know how sometimes you do things without thinking much about the implications of what you do.'

'Yes.'

She persevered. 'So now I'm saying sorry to you. I'm apologising. And . . .' She tried to look him in the eye, but his gaze slipped away, as it often did. 'And I really think that you should accept my apology.'

A customer pushed open the door and made her way over to the pasta shelves.

'Eddie?'

'All right. I accept your apology.'

'Thank you.' Isabel dusted her hands on her apron. Another impulse seized her. 'And why don't you come and have supper with Jamie and me this evening? Nothing grand. Kitchen supper.'

At first he did not know how to respond to this suggestion. She saw him hesitating, and she pressed home the invitation. 'Come on, Eddie. We've known one another a long time and you've never been round to the house. Not once. You like Jamie, don't you?'

'Jamie? I like him.'

'Well then, say yes.'

'All right. I'll come.' He paused. 'And thanks. Thank you for inviting me.'

Isabel slightly regretted the invitation, not because she did not want to entertain Eddie, but because it meant that she would lose an evening that she had mentally earmarked for work. There were still four weeks before she would need to send the next issue of the *Review* off to the printers, but she knew from past experience how quickly those weeks could pass. What she wanted to avoid was a frantic last few days during which she would have to deal with matters that could have been sorted out well in advance. But today could be written off – a day devoted to Cat's interests, and Eddie surely came into that category.

Jamie was in the house when she got home. He had arrived at four and had taken over Charlie duties from Grace, though not without a battle, it seemed.

'She was very unwilling to go,' he complained to Isabel. 'She more or less implied that I was being disruptive.'

Isabel grimaced. 'You're only his father, after all.'

Jamie smiled. He did not bear grudges. 'That's more or less what I said. Anyway, Charlie and I have been having a great time.' He pointed to a clutter of toy vehicles on the floor: a fire engine, a tractor. 'He's going to be a mechanic, I think. Or an engineer.'

Charlie started to crawl away, and Isabel intercepted him. 'Not a musician?'

'Who would be a musician?' Jamie said, beginning to pick up the toys. 'Years of practising. Awful hours. No money . . .'

Isabel was cuddling Charlie. 'But you do what you love doing,' she said over her shoulder. 'How many people can say that?'

'Quite a few, I suspect,' said Jamie. 'Most doctors like doctoring, don't they? And most lawyers like arguing – or at least the ones I know do. And you hear about pilots saying that they get a real high from being up there above the clouds. And you . . .'

He placed the toys in a large open hamper filled with Charlie's things: soft animals, a teddy in a kilt, building blocks in primary colours – a world of shapes, surfaces, textures. Then he stood up. Charlie was nestling into the nape of her neck, his back turned to his father, his mother's arms about him. Jamie stepped forward; his face was close to Isabel's and she looked at him in surprise. He kissed her suddenly, with an urgent passion. 'I love you very much,' he said.

Her pleasure showed. 'Well, thank you, and I love you too.'

'Let's go away,' he said. 'You, me. Charlie. Let's just go away.'

His eyes were locked into hers. She bent forward again and kissed him lightly on the cheek. 'Where?' she asked. 'Go where?'

It was as if he had expected her to say no and was excited to find her saying yes. 'Anywhere you like,' he said. 'Somewhere in the west. Ireland even.'

'When?'

'Tomorrow morning.'

She moved away. Charlie was becoming heavy. 'We can't. There's the delicatessen. Remember? And you're busy this week, aren't you? I thought you said that you had the Scottish Chamber Orchestra.'

'We've both got things on,' he said. 'But Charlie's free.'

Isabel laughed. 'They get social diaries at a very early age these days,' she said. 'I was reading about some mothers in a fashionable part of London who keep social diaries for their children. The kids have dinner parties. Dancing lessons. And so on.'

'I want Charlie to learn Scottish country dancing,' said Jamie. 'He's almost old enough. Once he can walk properly.'

They both laughed. Then Isabel looked at her watch. 'We'll have to get Charlie settled in good time,' she said. 'Eddie's coming for dinner.'

Jamie took Charlie from her. The little boy held on to her blouse, reluctant to let go. She laid a hand gently over his tightened fist; the tension went out of it and his fingers opened.

'Bath time,' said Jamie. 'Why do you think they love bath time so much?'

'It's a return to the womb,' said Isabel. 'It's how we felt once and how we want to feel again.'

She had not thought about it, but it sounded right, and was probably true. The living of our lives involved loss; loss at every point. Perhaps Charlie really did remember the comfort of the womb; it was not all that long ago, in his case. And what did she want to recover? Did she want her mother back, her sainted American mother? Or her father? Or the feeling of freedom and excitement she had experienced when first she went to Cambridge?

She looked at Jamie as he left the room, heading upstairs to the bath that he would run for Charlie. There would come a time, no doubt, when she would think back to these moments and regret them; not in the sense of wishing they had never been, but regret them in the sense of wishing them back into existence.

She followed Jamie upstairs. A line came to her, a snatch of poetry: John Betjeman, of all people, a snuffly romantic, who could write about love, though, with heart-stopping effect.

There had been his Irish Unionist's farewell to the woman he loved; Irish Unionists, she thought, have not had their fair share of poetry – all the best lines were claimed by the republican-minded Irish. But Irish Unionists fell in love and suffered for love in the same way as everybody else did, and could feel that they were in danger of drowning in love, as anybody could, and as she felt now.

8

Eddie seemed a different person. The blue jeans had been replaced with black ones – formal wear, thought Isabel wryly – and the tee-shirt had yielded to a roll-top sweater in the green that Isabel's father had always described as British Racing. His face looked scrubbed, his hair combed and damp, as if freshly sprinkled with water.

'You're looking very smart, Eddie,' she said as she let him in the front door.

The compliment pleased him. He had looked uncertain when she had opened the door; now he smiled.

'I saw a fox, you know,' he said as he stepped into the hall. 'Right outside. On the path. That far away from me. Just that far.'

'Brother Fox,' said Isabel. 'He lives somewhere around here. We are in his territory. Did he look at you?'

Eddie nodded. 'He didn't seem frightened. He looked at me like this.' And here he made a face, narrowing his eyes. How like Brother Fox he looks, thought Isabel.

'He watches us,' said Isabel. 'And he keeps other, less friendly foxes away.' She paused. 'Sometimes I wish I could introduce him to the Duke of Buccleuch. He has a fox hunt, you know, down in the Borders. They need to talk.'

Eddie looked at Isabel, puzzled; she said some very strange things, he thought. And her house . . . he looked about in awe.

'You've got a big place,' he said.

She thought of Eddie's circumstances. Cat had said something once about where he lived; he was still with his parents somewhere, she believed, somewhere down off Leith Walk. Eddie's parents were elderly, she now remembered; he had been something of an afterthought.

'It's just a house,' she said.

He looked at her, as if expecting her to say something more.

'I mean, I'm used to it,' she went on. 'I suppose it's too large for me, but I'm just used to it. I don't think of it as being big.' She sounded foolish; she should have said nothing. Those who live in big houses, she thought, should not apologise; it only makes matters worse.

'I wouldn't know what to do in a place like this,' said Eddie. 'I'd get lost.'

'Well, maybe.' She touched Eddie's arm lightly. 'Charlie would like to see you, I think. He's just had his bath. Jamie's with him.'

She led him upstairs. Eddie glanced at the paintings on the stair and on the landing. 'Are these all . . . all real?'

She smiled. 'Yes, they're real. If you mean they're actual paintings. Real paint. Not prints.'

'That's what I meant.'

They were standing in front of a Peploe landscape. In the background she heard Charlie gurgling as Jamie uttered some nonsensical mantra. Eddie reached out as if to touch the painting, but checked himself.

'You can touch it if you like,' said Isabel. 'It's quite dry now.'

'Why are the hills blue like that?' asked Eddie.

She thought: yes, that is a reasonable question to ask of the colourists, who saw the world in strong colours. Mull, and its hills, were blue, seen from the blue shores of Iona. 'Because hills are often blue. Look at them. It's the effect of the light.'

Eddie looked more closely at the picture. 'Is this worth a lot of money?' he asked.

Isabel was momentarily taken aback. But she quickly recovered. She would have to be honest. 'Yes, anything by Peploe is quite expensive these days. He's a very highly sought-after artist. That's what determines the price. Like Picasso. There's nothing very special in a Picasso drawing, say, but it will still cost an awful lot of money.'

'How much?' asked Eddie.

'Picasso? Oh, well a drawing – a few lines dashed off on a sheet of paper – might be ten thousand pounds.'

'No, not that. This painting here. This Pep . . . Peploe.'

Isabel laughed, as much to cover her embarrassment as for any other reason. 'I don't think you should ask questions like that, Eddie. People don't . . . don't expect to be asked what things cost.'

She spoke gently, but her words silenced him. He looked down at the floor, and she immediately regretted what she had said.

She felt that she needed to explain. 'Sorry, Eddie. You can ask me; of course you can ask me. It's just that . . . well, you wouldn't normally ask somebody else, somebody whom you didn't really know.'

He bit his lip.

'I'll tell you, if you like. Of course I'll tell you. Although . . .'

102

What would be the effect of his knowing? Envy? 'I didn't buy that painting; it belonged to my father. And he didn't pay a great deal for it. Not in those days.'

He was still looking at the floor. She reached out and held his arm. 'All right. If that went into an auction now, it would fetch over one hundred thousand pounds. That's what somebody told me, anyway.'

He looked up sharply. The offence that he had taken at her mild censure was now replaced by astonishment. 'You could sell it for that? For over a hundred thousand?'

She explained that she did not want to sell it.

'Why not? Think what you could do with a hundred thousand pounds.'

'Frankly, I can't think of anything I'd spend it on. What do I need? I don't want a new car. I've got a house. I'm lucky. I don't need a hundred thousand pounds.'

She spoke freely, but as the words came out, again she felt that she was making a mistake. She did not need anything, but he did. He had no car, she assumed; and he certainly did not own a flat. I'm making it worse, she thought. But no, Eddie had not taken it in that way at all; he was thinking of something else. 'So is that why you gave that man the cheese this afternoon? Because you don't need to worry about money?'

She thought about this. He was probably right. If you had enough, you were more likely to be liberal to others; except, of course, as was always the case, for some. 'Possibly,' she said.

'And what if I came to you and said, "Isabel, please give me five hundred pounds." What if I said that? Would you?'

She studied his expression, trying to work out whether he was asking for money. She decided that he was not.

'I'd give it to you. But I'd probably ask you first why you needed it. If you were in trouble, of course I'd give it to you.'

'Not lend it?'

'No. I'd give it.'

She watched him. His mouth twitched slightly; just slightly, at the edges of the lips. 'Eddie? Do you need five hundred pounds? Is that what you're telling me?'

She observed the pupils of his eyes; dark dots, but with light in them. She noticed that he had a mole, a tiny mole, just below his ear. Otherwise, he was perfect.

His lips parted, a tiny bit of spittle. He mouthed the word *yes*.

She whispered, as she did not want Jamie to hear, and she suddenly knew that Jamie was listening from Charlie's room, through the open door.

'Are you in trouble, Eddie?'

He said nothing, but his head moved slightly: a nod.

'And will you tell me what it is?'

Again a movement of the head, this time a shaking.

She made up her mind. Five hundred pounds was very little to her and would obviously make a big difference to Eddie in his difficulties, whatever they were. A fine? She thought that unlikely. Eddie was too timid to get into trouble with the law. Drugs? Debts to a pusher? There was no sign that he used any-thing, and she thought it unlikely; Cat had told her that he had expressed strong views against drugs some months before. So what did that leave?

She leaned forward. 'Will you need more? If I give you five hundred pounds, will you come back and ask for more?'

He began to look indignant, but then stopped himself. 'No,' he said quietly. 'That's all I need.'

She made her mind up. 'All right. We can get the money from the bank tomorrow.'

She did not expect effusive thanks, and did not get them. But there was a whispered *thank you* as they went into Charlie's room. Jamie was standing there, holding Charlie in his sleeper suit. He glanced at Eddie and nodded; then looked at Isabel. She let nothing pass between them, no acknowledgement of what had happened on the landing. It's between Eddie and me, she thought. Private business. Eddie had told her not to give cheese away; would Jamie tell her not to give money away? It's mine, she thought – although the cheese, strictly speaking, was not.

Charlie saw Eddie and gave a welcoming gurgle.

'He likes you,' said Jamie.

'Babies do,' said Eddie. 'My mum says . . .' He trailed off.

'She says what?' asked Isabel.

'She says they go by smell,' said Eddie.

Isabel took Charlie out of Jamie's arms and passed him over to Eddie. 'Jamie smells good,' she said. 'And I'm sure you do as well. Here.'

Eddie recoiled at first, in fright, but checked himself. He was awkward, uncertain precisely where to place his arms, but Charlie helped by latching on to his sweater.

'Support him,' said Isabel, taking hold of Eddie's right forearm. Bony. Was he eating properly? If he lived with his parents, then surely his mother should watch out for that. Or Cat should. She was his employer; she should notice these things. And there was no shortage of food in a delicatessen.

'You're nice and thin, Eddie,' she said, patting the arm she had briefly held.

'That's because he walks everywhere,' Jamie chipped in. 'You do, don't you, Eddie?'

105

Eddie nodded. 'It's quicker,' he said.

'But you don't want to be too thin,' said Isabel.

Jamie reached forward to tickle Charlie under the chin. 'What do they say? You can never be too thin, nor too rich.'

'Isabel's too rich,' said Eddie. 'She just said so.'

There was a silence, and Charlie, surprised, looked over Eddie's shoulder at the people standing around him: there had been gurgles, he thought, those sounds that they made, and now nothing.

Yet the dinner went well, at least until just before the end. Eddie was relaxed, and Isabel could tell that he enjoyed Jamie's company. From the other side of the table, he looked at Jamie with a bright-eyed admiration, she thought, and this made her smile; many people looked at Jamie that way, and yet he did not appear to notice, or, if he was aware of it, did not think anything of it. *The blessed will not care what angle they are regarded from, having nothing to hide*: the line from 'In Praise of Limestone' came to her unbidden – WHA again! But it was so apt.

They ate salmon terrine, followed by a risotto, from a recipe which Isabel had taken from Mary Contini's book, and then grapes. Jamie wanted coffee, but Isabel and Eddie did not; so Isabel made a small espresso for Jamie, and while she was doing this, the two of them at the table and she at the worktop, Eddie said: 'I can hypnotise people now.'

Jamie looked at him oddly, like an older brother faced with a younger sibling who has made a bragging claim. 'Oh yes? Since when?'

'Since a week ago,' said Eddie. 'Officially. I got my certificate then. My Part One certificate. I still have to do Part Two and Part Three.'

Jamie appeared puzzled, and Eddie explained about his

course. 'It's hard work,' he said. 'Quite a few people dropped out.'

'Well done, Eddie,' said Isabel. 'You must be pleased—'

'Hypnotise me, then,' Jamie interjected.

Eddie looked at him anxiously. 'You serious?'

Jamie glanced at Isabel. She wanted to shake her head, to say no, but could not; she was careful about telling him what he could or could not do. She was not his mother. He turned back to Eddie. 'Yes, why not? It would be interesting, don't you think, Isabel?'

'It's not a game,' said Eddie.

Isabel was concerned. She did not want Jamie to be hypnotised. She did not want anybody to be hypnotised in her kitchen. She would change the subject. 'Of course it's not. Not like one of those games you play after dinner. You know, the six degrees of separation game. Things like that. Can you get to the Pope through five friends?'

'Two,' said Jamie. 'In my case.'

Eddie looked blank.

'Right,' said Jamie. 'I know the cardinal, the one who lives over at Church Hill, in that house with the green copper dome. He must know the Pope. Two degrees of separation from me to the Pope.'

Isabel wanted to encourage this new line of discussion. 'So you're three degrees away from the Pope, Eddie. You know Jamie. Jamie knows the cardinal. The cardinal knows the Pope. Three degrees.'

'And the president of Bulgaria?' suggested Jamie.

Isabel frowned. 'I suspect that he has a lot of friends,' she said. 'So I suspect that we'd get there within six links.'

'He has a lot of friends?' asked Eddie. 'How do you know?'

Isabel shrugged her shoulders. Eddie could be very literal. 'In order to become president of anywhere, even Bulgaria, you have to have friends. You have to know lots of people and cultivate them. He'll be a networker, the president of Bulgaria. A big networker.'

She looked to Jamie for support, but he was looking at Eddie. The president of Bulgaria was not getting the attention he deserved. 'Go on, Eddie,' said Jamie. 'Hypnotise me. I'm ready. What do I have to do?'

'The president of Bulgaria,' Isabel said. 'Now let's think. I know Malcolm Rifkind, and he used to be Foreign Secretary. So, he may . . .'

'Do I just sit here?' asked Jamie. 'Do we need to turn the lights off?'

Eddie shook his head. They were sitting at the kitchen table, where casual meals were taken, and the lighting was low anyway. 'It's best not to be distracted,' he said. 'That's why it's sometimes a good idea to turn down the lights. But it's not very bright in here.' He stood up and moved round the table to sit down on the chair next to Jamie's. 'I'm going to sit here. You turn round a bit, so that you're looking at me.'

Isabel brought Jamie's cup of coffee over to the table and put it beside him. 'Are you going to drink this before you go under, or afterwards?'

He smiled, but said nothing, leaving the coffee untouched. She went back to her seat.

Eddie had fixed his gaze on Jamie. He leaned forward very slightly. 'I want you to listen to my voice. Just listen. Hear nothing else. All right?'

Jamie nodded.

'And as you listen to me, you're going to feel yourself getting drowsier and drowsier. Your eyelids will be getting heavier, like lead. That's it. And all the tension is going out of you. Flowing away. You can feel it going down your arms and out of your fingertips – draining away like water. That's right. Don't struggle against it.'

Eddie continued in this vein for a further five minutes. Jamie remained still, and Eddie did not take his eyes off him as he talked. If Isabel had looked at Jamie, she would have seen that a smile played about his lips; it was almost imperceptible, but a sign of what he was thinking. Yet she did not see this, because her own eyes were firmly closed. She was breathing deeply.

Jamie suddenly turned his head and looked at Isabel. He signalled to Eddie, who stopped what he was saying and followed Jamie's gaze. Eddie was silent for a few moments. Then: 'Isabel. I'm going to ask you to do something. Afterwards, I'm going to snap my fingers and when I do that you'll wake up. Do you understand?'

Isabel did not open her eyes, but she moved her head slightly to indicate assent.

'Right,' said Eddie, winking at Jamie. 'Now when I tell you to open your eyes, you'll see somebody come into the room. This is a person you really, really want to see. Somebody you know well and you want to see again. They'll come in just to say hallo and then they'll go out again. But you'll tell us who it is. All right?'

Again, Isabel nodded.

'So,' said Eddie. 'The door's opening. And your eyes too.'

Isabel's expression left no doubt that she was looking at somebody. Here was surprise, astonishment perhaps, and then an anguished cry: 'John. No, don't go. Don't go!'

Eddie rose to his feet. He snapped his fingers. Nothing happened. Then he snapped them again, more loudly this time. Isabel's head turned sharply.

Jamie leaned across the table and took her hand. 'Are you all right?'

Isabel looked about her. 'Of course I'm all right. Eddie, weren't you going to . . .'

'No,' said Eddie. He shifted uncomfortably in his seat, glancing anxiously at Jamie, as if for reassurance.

'Some other time,' said Jamie. 'Not now.' He picked up his small cup of espresso and drained it.

'I should be going home,' said Eddie awkwardly.

He said goodbye to Isabel quickly and Jamie showed him to the door. Then, returning to the kitchen, Jamie found Isabel facing him.

She looked bemused. 'Something happened, didn't it?'

He looked down at the floor. He felt embarrassed to speak about it, but he could hardly refuse to answer her question. 'He was trying to hypnotise me, but you somehow got in the way. You went under,' he said, 'like that. I remained wide awake, but you . . . It was very quick. I wondered whether to stop it, but I thought it might be risky.'

She gasped. 'I went under?'

'Yes. You must be very . . . what do they say? Susceptible?'

'And what happened?'

He looked embarrassed, and she caught her breath. 'Do you really want to know?'

This, she thought, is how a drunk must feel when he wakes up the next morning and has no recollection of the night before. What did I do? She felt instinctively for her clothing; it was still there. And surely Jamie would not have allowed

110

anything untoward to happen; he would have stopped her from disgracing herself.

'You saw John Liamor,' he said quietly. 'You saw him come into the room and you cried out to him.' He could tell that she was aghast. 'No, you didn't say very much. You just shouted out his name and told him not to go. That was all. Then Eddie clicked his fingers and you came out of it. Nothing more than that.'

She leaned forward, her head in her hands. She had tried so hard to forget John Liamor, the man she had married; the man who had broken her heart, once, twice, over and over again. He meant nothing to her now, nothing – consciously, at least.

'I'm not still in love with him,' she muttered.

Jamie came to her and put his arm about her. 'Of course you aren't. Of course.'

He had Cat to forget; he knew what an effort it cost. 'Let's think of the president of Bulgaria,' he said.

9

Not thinking about something can be hard, as Isabel discovered the next day. She had decided to put the incident in the kitchen out of her mind, but it kept coming back. Did she really want to see John Liamor again? Did he still mean something to her? Did what one said under hypnosis have anything to do with what really was going on in the subconscious mind? Surely the mind was full of all sorts of old memories that were really of no significance for how one felt; they merely knocked about in some deep region, like the detritus at the bottom of a lake. And if they surfaced from time to time, that did not mean very much.

At first it was awkward with Eddie. He avoided her when he came into the delicatessen the next morning, but Isabel made a point of speaking to him. 'Eddie, what happened last night is nothing. I don't feel bad about it, and neither should you.' She took his arm. Again that feeling of thinness. 'Don't look away from me, Eddie. Come on now.'

'I'm really sorry,' he mumbled.

She reached out and put her hand against his cheek. He looked at her in surprise. 'Come on, Eddie. You don't have to be sorry about anything. John Liamor was my husband. I shouted out his name because I obviously still think about him subconsciously. Maybe I still care for him. I thought I didn't.'

She moved her hand away, and she felt him relax. She let go of his arm. Holding Eddie was like holding a cat who does not want to be held.

'I'm still sorry,' he said. 'They told us that we should be careful about what we did with it.'

She laughed. 'Well, that's one way of learning that. And there was no harm done anyway.'

He rubbed the place on his arm where she had held him, as if he had been bruised. 'You seemed very upset about seeing him. About seeing John Whatsisname.'

'He hurt me,' said Isabel.

Eddie looked up sharply. 'Beat you?'

'Not that. No. But there are lots of other ways of being hurt. And they can be as bad.'

Eddie was silent. I could say something now, she thought. I could say to him: I know that you've been hurt too, badly. But she did not. Instead, she said, 'Are you all right, Eddie? You know that I'm going to go down to the bank today.' She looked at her watch. 'In fact, I've got two things I have to do. Do you mind being in charge for a while a bit later on?'

He did not. But he did not say anything about the bank, and so Isabel persisted. 'I'm going to get that money I promised you. Remember?' She paused, watching him. He bit his lip. 'You said you were in trouble, Eddie. Are you sure that you don't want to tell me what it is?'

'I don't,' he muttered.

'All right. You don't need to. But if you change your mind

about that and want to talk to me, I promise you that I wouldn't tell anybody else. All right?'

He nodded his assent and crossed the room to get his apron from its hook. One act, she thought; one act of violence, one act of callous gratification, and a young life was made into this.

The bank was the simple part. They had the money ready for her in a white envelope and slipped it to her across the broad wooden desk. She wondered whether people who worked in banks thought about what their clients did with their money, or whether such interest quickly faded. Money was very mundane, really, and the question of who had what was hardly riveting. Or did she feel that way, she asked herself, because she had more than most? She felt no envy when she read, as one occasionally did, of people earning large salaries or bonuses. But others hated this, and muttered darkly about higher taxes and obscene profits. What was obscene about earning a lot of money? One could not put that reaction entirely down to simple envy; there must be something more to it. Unfairness, perhaps. It was unfair that one should have so much when so many had so little. And it was, she thought. In which case, should she divest herself further? She gave a lot to various causes, and one of these charities had written to her recently in a way which spoke of an appeal – a very tactfully put appeal, but an appeal none the less.

She caught a taxi in Charlotte Square and gave the address of the Café Sardi, a small Italian restaurant in the university area. It had been convenient for the old medical school before it moved out to the new infirmary, and there were still some doctors who used it to meet for lunch. He had to be in town, he said, and they could meet there.

114

She was the first to arrive, and was led to a table near the window that gave her a view over the road to Sandy Bell's. She looked up. There was a picture of Hamish Henderson on the wall of the restaurant; he had been an habitué of Sandy Bell's all those years ago and must have eaten here too. She had heard him singing in Sandy Bell's from time to time, that tireless collector of Scottish folk songs with his great lumbering frame and his toothy smile.

She sought to invoke the memory. Yes, the first time she had heard him he had sung 'Freedom Come All Ye' while she sat at a table at the back of the pub with her friends, utterly arrested, unable to do anything but watch that curious rumpled figure and hear the words that cut into the air like the punch of a fist: *Nae mair will our bonnie callants / Merch tae wer when our braggarts crousely craw.* No more will Scottish boys march off to war to the skirl of the pipes. And at the end she had cried; she had been unable to say why, beyond feeling that what she had witnessed was a heartfelt apology for what Scotland had done to the world as part of the British Empire, for all the humiliation of imperialism.

She was thinking of this when Dr Norrie Brown came in. She knew it was him from the way he hesitated at the door, looking for someone he did not know; and he knew it was her from the way she sat there waiting for somebody similarly unknown to her.

'Isabel Dalhousie?'

She reached out and shook his hand. He sat down opposite her and looked at her appraisingly. There was no attempt to conceal what he was doing; he was taking her measure. She blushed.

'I'm terribly sorry,' he said. 'Tactless of me. I can't help it,

I'm afraid. When I meet somebody for the first time, I've got into the habit of looking at them as if they're a new patient. I don't quite take the blood pressure, but I do sum things up.'

She smiled. There was a pleasant frankness about the way he spoke, and she liked the look of him too. He was in his mid-thirties, she decided; open-faced, uncomplicated. A straightforward doctor.

'Oh well,' she said. 'We all look at others according to our calling. I have a lawyer friend who immediately examines people as if they're in the witness box. And my hairdresser looks out of the window and comments on the hair of people going past. Bad hair day. That sort of thing!'

He reached for the menu. 'I assure you, you look quite well. And so I conclude that you don't want to consult me professionally.'

'Certainly not.'

He glanced at the menu. 'So? Do you mind if I ask why you got in touch? You said it was to do with a mutual friend.'

'Yes,' she said. 'Marcus Moncrieff.'

He replaced the menu on the table. 'Oh. Marcus.'

'Yes. I know his wife, you see. Not very well, but enough to know that she's terribly worried about him.'

He watched her as she spoke. The openness she had detected earlier on was being replaced, she thought, by a marked guardedness.

'Marcus is pretty low, is he? I haven't seen him for a month or so; I must go round. I take it that it's the . . .'

'Disgrace?'

'You could call it that. And I suppose that's what it was.'

The waitress came and took their order. Norrie, she noticed,

116

chose a salad and a diet drink. 'I'm training as a gastroenterologist now,' he said. 'I see what people put in their stomachs. It's enough to put one off eating altogether.'

She smiled. 'But you won't disapprove of what I have.'

He laughed. 'Probably. But I won't say anything. An Italian diet is reasonably healthy, anyway. It's the stuff they eat in Glasgow that does the damage. The fries. The red meat. The fried fish. My cardiac colleagues could keep you entertained for hours on the subject.'

Isabel steered the conversation back to Marcus. 'The incident,' she began. 'The incident that led to the complaint. Do you think it was his fault?'

Norrie said nothing for a moment, but fingered the stem of an empty glass in front of him. When he eventually spoke, he seemed to be choosing his words with care. 'The finding against him was clear,' he said. 'He was negligent. The figures on the dosage were far too high. He should have checked. He didn't.'

'Where did those figures come from?'

'From the lab.'

Isabel watched Norrie carefully. His manner was very matter-of-fact, as if he were relating everyday events, rather than ones that had brought a career to an end.

'And what did you think? What did you think of the figures?'

Again he took his time to answer, and again, when he did, his words were careful. 'I just took note of them and passed them on.'

'That's all?'

He held her gaze. He neither blinked, nor looked away. 'It wasn't for me to say anything. I was – am – a junior doctor. I came to medicine late, you see. I did a degree in engineering and then changed my mind. It's going to be some time before I catch up.'

'It wasn't for you to say anything?'

'No. That's what I've just told you.'

She persisted. 'Even if you thought they were high?'

His self-controlled manner slipped a little. 'Listen,' he said, an edge appearing in his voice. 'I didn't have a clue.'

She made a calming gesture with a hand. 'All right. Sorry, I'm not accusing you of anything. I just think that Marcus may have been harshly treated. I was hoping that we could find out something which puts him in a better light.'

This remark seemed to take him by surprise. 'Harshly treated?'

She explained that she felt that a momentary lapse of judgement should not, in her view, end a career. Anybody could make a mistake – indeed everybody made mistakes. But that did not make them culpable. 'So,' she concluded. 'I was wondering whether I could come up with something that could help him to establish that he was not blameworthy. I wondered if I could get him off this awful hook of blame.'

Norrie stared at her, almost incredulously. 'You want it reopened?'

'Yes,' said Isabel. 'If need be.'

The waitress now brought his salad and Isabel's pasta, and laid the plates before them. Norrie took up a fork and began to pick at the meal. 'If I were you,' he said quietly, 'I'd leave well enough alone. Don't try to open anything up. Just don't.'

Isabel speared a shell of pasta with her fork, and then another. 'But if there is anything which could help him,' she said, 'surely it should be brought up.'

118

Norrie seemed to weigh this for a while. 'All right,' he said at last. 'If I tell you something, will you give me your word that you won't use it publicly in any way?'

She considered this. It would not be easy to give an assurance of confidentiality if he was going to come up with some information that could exculpate Marcus. But if she did not agree, then she would not hear it. She decided that she had no alternative.

'Very well. I give you my word. Even if it's going to hamper me.'

'It won't hamper you,' Norrie said quickly. 'And it won't be to Marcus's disadvantage. Quite the opposite.'

'I don't see—'

But he cut her short. He had abandoned his salad now, and there was light in his eyes. 'Marcus Moncrieff is even more guilty than you imagine. He got off lightly.'

She sat back in her seat. 'I don't see—'

'No,' he said quickly. 'You don't, do you? You don't because you don't know the first thing about it. Sorry to be so frank, but these things are very complex. The truth of the matter, you see, is that *I* warned him that the figures were high. *I* said to him that he should go and check the figures and see whether they really reflected what the patient had taken. And he didn't. He said no, it wasn't necessary. And then I spoke to him a second time, and asked him to note my reservations, but he told me not to be such a fusspot and he didn't note anything.'

He attacked his salad. 'So, you see,' he said. 'Not so simple. If that had come out at the enquiry it would have looked even worse for him.'

'But you didn't mention it?'

'No. I wasn't even asked to make a statement. I kept quiet. I didn't want things to get even worse for him. He's a good doctor, you see.'

'You protected him?'

He stared at her. 'You could put it that way. But let me say something else. If you mention this at all, and in particular if you suggest to anybody that I protected him, I shall simply deny that this conversation took place.'

She was puzzled. 'Then why tell me?'

'To protect him again,' he said. 'To protect him from you.' He pointed at her with his fork, on which half an olive was balanced. The olive tumbled down into the thick of the salad and was lost. 'The last thing he needs is anybody opening up the whole can of worms. If you're really concerned for him, then you'll back off now that you know you only risk making it worse.'

They both ate in silence for a while. Then Norrie spoke again. 'And there's another thing which nobody knows. In the case of the second patient, there was nothing wrong with the figures from the lab. And the dosage was not nearly as high. Yet the lab report, when it came to be looked at again, had much higher figures. Somebody had altered them.'

He looked at her knowingly.

'You're saying that Marcus did?'

'Well, I didn't change them,' he said.

'And you didn't do anything about it?'

'By then it was too late. I only noticed it when the whole thing started to be investigated.'

It did not make sense to Isabel. She could understand sloppiness and not bothering to check up on suspect figures, but why should Marcus have deliberately falsified data?

Norrie sensed the reasons for her puzzlement. 'Because he

didn't want the drug to be compromised,' he said. 'Because he didn't want its use to be stopped because of some awkward side effects at relatively low doses. If these things happened with absolutely sky-high doses, then that would not be the fault of the drug, it would be a sort of freak occurrence – the sort of risk that people will live with precisely because hardly anybody is ever going to swallow enough of the stuff for that sort of thing to happen.'

Isabel digested this. It certainly made sense. But why, she wondered, would he have such a stake in the continued use of the drug?

Norrie put down his fork; he had finished his salad. A small piece of dark lettuce had stuck to the front of his teeth and his tongue moved round as he tried to dislodge it, while Isabel stared in awful fascination.

'Excuse me,' he said, picking at his teeth with a fingernail. 'There. That's better. What do they say about these things? Follow the money. Isn't that it?'

'He had a financial interest in the company?'

'Not directly,' said Norrie. 'He wouldn't have had shares – that would have been too obvious. But that same company had backed his research. He was beholden to them. He probably wanted them to back him in the future. So . . .'

Isabel listened carefully. What was occupying her now was the question of why Norrie should have so readily covered for Marcus. Was this the way the medical profession looked after its own? She had been under the impression that all that had changed. It was difficult to understand.

'But what I can't work out,' she said, 'is this: why did you not say something? Why did you not reveal your suspicions that he had actually gone so far as to change data?'

Norrie pushed his plate away from him and glanced at his watch. 'I'm going to have to dash,' he said. 'I'm doing a couple of endoscopies this afternoon in an hour or so.' He paused, as if weighing whether to say something. Then he did. 'All right, bearing in mind that this conversation is completely deniable: Marcus Moncrieff is my uncle. He's my mother's brother.'

He looked at her in a way that seemed to her to say: You are admitted to a conspiracy; I think you understand. Then he signalled to the waitress to bring the bill.

'Edinburgh's a bit like that,' he said.

10

Jamie was playing that evening at the Festival Theatre. Scottish Opera was doing *Don Pasquale*, and although Isabel had seen the production when they had first performed it in Glasgow, she had been invited to the opera, and a reception beforehand, by Turcan Connel, the firm of lawyers who represented her in such legal business as she had. It was one of their partners, Simon Mackintosh, who had purchased the *Review of Applied Ethics* on her behalf the previous year, and he said that this transaction entitled her to at least some corporate hospitality.

Champagne was served in one of the suites alongside the grand circle. Isabel saw that she knew a number of the guests, but for some reason she did not feel much like socialising, so busied herself looking at the framed theatrical memorabilia on the wall. There was the programme for a concert by Harry Lauder, the Scottish vaudeville artist of the 1920s, with a picture of the famous bekilted figure with one of the twisted walking sticks that became his trademark. He had opened the show with 'Will Ye Stop Your Tickling, Jock' and had ended it with 'Keep Right On to the End of the Road'. Isabel smiled; her father had loved Harry Lauder and had sung his songs to

Isabel and her brother when they were children. 'Keep Right On to the End of the Road' moved her still, mawkish though the words were in cold print. *Every road through life is a long, long road / Filled with joys and sorrow too.* Trite? Yes, it was, but then the truth was often trite, and nonetheless true for that. And had Harry Lauder not sung those lines on the very day that he heard of the death of his only son in the trenches of France? And he had insisted on going on stage to sing it when his heart must have been broken within him. People did that back then. They were brave.

Or were they too brave, Isabel wondered; too brave, with the result that they were imposed upon in the name of vainglorious patriotism, chauvinism, easily led to the slaughter? Should one be brave about the loss of one's only son, or should one break down and weep for the waste, the pointlessness of the loss; rail against the whole monstrous system that sent young men off in droves to climb up those ladders and stumble through the mud into veils of machine-gun fire? Why should anyone be brave about that?

She remembered the Latin teacher at school translating '*Dulce et decorum est pro patria mori*' – it is a sweet and decorous thing to die for one's country. 'Horace, girls,' she said. 'That's from Horace's *Odes*. Horace was a poet who wrote about the pleasures of living in the country.'

'Who died for his country?' asked one of the girls.

And the teacher had said, 'No. He was talking about other people.' And left it at that.

She turned away from the Lauder programme and raised her champagne glass to her lips. Simon, who was standing with a knot of people near the door, saw her and came across to speak to her.

'Do you want to meet anybody?' he asked.

'No. Not really.'

He smiled. 'I thought so. I know how you feel. Has it been one of those days?'

Isabel took another sip of champagne. 'Yes,' she said. 'But this helps.'

'The *Review*? Problems with that?'

Isabel shook her head. 'I'm looking after Cat's delicatessen, and I was worked off my feet. Then I had lunch with some-body who revealed something which made me think. Nothing personal, but something which, well, which shocked me. So I just feel a bit . . .'

Simon put a finger to his lips. 'You don't need to tell me,' he said. 'I understand. Why don't you just slip through to your seat. We won't be offended. Catriona will come through in a moment and sit next to you.'

Isabel did as he suggested and left the reception to find her way to her seat in the grand circle. The house was filling up, and there was that low hum of conversation that precedes the curtain: people waved to one another here and there, pro-grammes were studied in the half-light, jackets were taken off and draped around the backs of seats.

Isabel read the biographies in her programme. There was a Russian tenor, appearing in Scotland for the first time; there was a young singer fresh out of the Royal Scottish Academy in Glasgow; Don Pasquale himself had sung the role at Covent Garden and was shortly going off to Sydney. She turned to the summary; it was always helpful to refresh one's memory as to the argument of an opera. 'Don Pasquale plans for Ernesto to marry a candidate of his choice, but Ernesto is really in love with Norina . . .' Her attention wandered, and she looked about her. The man in the seat in front of her was whispering to his wife, pointing, discreetly enough, to a couple at the other end of the row. Isabel wondered what that was about. The wife shook her head. Disapproval? Or misidentification?

Her gaze wandered. Over to her right, she saw her friends Willy and Vanessa Prosser; they had not seen her, but she would go and have a word with them in the interval. And behind them . . . she stopped. A few seats away from her, but two rows behind, was Nick Smart – and he was looking directly at her.

She could hardly pretend not to see him, as she was half-turned in her seat and looking directly at him. So she lifted a hand and gave him a half-hearted wave. He smiled, and rose to his feet. He was making his way over to speak to her.

He crouched down in the aisle, beside her seat. 'How nice to see you,' he said.

'Yes. Likewise.' She sounded forced, she could tell. And so could he, she imagined.

'You enjoy Donizetti?'

'Of course. Yes. I've seen this production in Glasgow.'

He had seen it at the Met.

'Ah.'

'Yes. And on the evening I saw it,' he continued, 'the singer in the title role had an allergic attack – during the final interval. Somebody popped his head round the curtain and said, "Give us four minutes, ladies and gentlemen." That's all they needed to get the understudy into his costume and push him on. Four minutes. And he sang beautifully. Brought the house down at the end.'

'My goodness.'

'Yes.' He had rolled his programme up and was tapping it

gently on the back of the seat in front of Isabel. She noticed that he was wearing a velvet jacket and that the cuffs of his shirt were secured with fancy cuff-links: a flash of gold. 'Tell me, how's Jamie?'

'He's playing tonight.'

'Yes, I know. I'm seeing him later.'

She felt a sudden lightness in her stomach; a strange sensation, almost like that which one experiences when driving a car over a hump. And then an emptiness.

'Yes,' he said. 'Later.' He looked at his watch. 'Well, I guess I'd better get back to my seat. It'll be starting in a moment.'

She heard herself mutter something, but she did not look at him. Her eyes were fixed on the curtains of the stage, but she was not taking them in. Catriona Mackintosh and her fellow guests had joined her now, and Isabel greeted Catriona, but in a distracted way.

'Are you all right?' whispered Catriona. 'Simon said you were feeling a bit low.'

Far more now, thought Isabel. 'No, I'm all right. A bit tired.'

'I won't notice if you drop off,' said Catriona.

There was little chance of that, thought Isabel. Where was he seeing him? And why had Jamie not mentioned it to her? She went over in her mind exactly what he had said about this evening. She had assumed that he was coming back to the house – he usually did on a Wednesday. In fact, he spent few evenings at his flat these days; sometimes he went there when he taught late at the Academy or when there was a concert on that side of town, but that was rare.

From where she was sitting she could, by leaning forward, see into the orchestra pit. She had not done so before now, because she had been reading the programme. Now she did, and she saw him sitting almost under the ledge of the stage. He looked up, but he could not see her; looking up into the theatre from down there one would see only black, just a sea of darkness behind the lights shining down upon the stage. He moved the neck of the bassoon, swivelling it round, and slipped the reed into his mouth to soften it. She saw all this. You are mine, she thought. You are mine.

After the performance she lingered in the glass-fronted foyer at the entrance to the theatre. There was a large throng of people; off to the side, the bar did roaring business. People were talking, laughing at shared jokes, struggling into coats. Taxis lined up in the street outside; the occasional chauffeur-driven car, its engine purring, its driver casting his eye anxiously over the crowd; a bus to take a group of people back to Stirling; a school outing congregating just outside the door, shepherded by a pair of teachers who had the look that teachers always have on such occasions – that counting look.

Isabel suddenly felt very lonely. There was nobody else, she thought, standing by herself; everybody was with somebody. She looked at her watch, more to give herself something to do than to find out the time. Jamie had said nothing about meeting her afterwards, and yet they usually did. He would suddenly materialise, carrying his bassoon case, and they would leave the concert hall together; except last time at the Queen's Hall, when he had gone for a drink with Nick Smart, and this time, she assumed, when he was planning to do the same.

She made up her mind. She would not wait for him; she would go home and relieve Grace of her babysitting duties. She had been carrying her coat over her arm, and now she slipped into it and began to button it up.

'There you are.' It was Jamie. He looked flushed, as if he had run round from the stage door at the side of the theatre.

She was not sure what to say. She was relieved to see him, but what about Nick?

He put his bassoon case down on the ground and reached forward to kiss Isabel on the cheek. 'I hope you liked it. I thought that it was the best performance of it they've done. That Russian has a fantastic voice.'

She agreed. He did.

'Look,' said Jamie, glancing at his watch. 'I have to see somebody about something. Do you mind? I'll go back to my flat afterwards, as I'm teaching down there tomorrow morning.'

She had that feeling again. It was somewhere in her chest. 'See somebody?'

He reached down to pick up his bassoon case. So that he does not have to look me in the eye, she thought. 'Yes,' he said. 'Nothing important. Music stuff.'

'Of course.' She tried to keep her voice even. How well do I really know him? Not well. 'I'd better go. Grace is looking after *our son*.' She stressed the last words, which was petty, and not what she had intended to do. He noticed, though.

'Isabel . . .'

'No. It's all right. I'll see you tomorrow.'

She moved towards the door. She hoped that he would run after her, would stop her leaving, but he did not, or not immediately. She had walked only as far as Nicholson Square, though, when he caught up with her.

'Isabel!'

She continued to walk, but he grabbed the sleeve of her coat and pulled her towards him. The strength of his tug almost made her trip, but she righted herself.

'Please leave me.'

'No. I won't. What's wrong?'

She drew in her breath. 'Leave me, you have to go and meet Nick Smart.'

He stared at her in astonishment. 'Who?'

'Nick. That composer. The one we met at the Queen's Hall.'

He frowned. 'But I'm not. I'm meant to be seeing Tom Martin. He's got the music for a recording we're doing for Paul Baxter. Delphian Records. You've met him.'

She tried to remember what Nick had said. 'I'm seeing him later.' Later that evening, or . . . People used the word later in different ways. Later could be next week, for all she knew.

She turned to him. Jamie was looking at her with a puzzled, almost hurt expression, and she knew at once that she had made a mistake.

'I'm sorry—' she began.

But he interrupted her. 'Why did you think I was going to meet Nick? What gave you that idea?'

She realised that there was an implicit accusation in what she had said; an accusation that could be devastating.

'He spoke to me before the curtain went up,' she said. 'He said he'd be seeing you later.'

He said nothing for a moment. He had been carrying his bassoon case, but had put it down when he had seized her. Now he picked it up with one hand and linked his other arm through hers.

'Let's walk.'

She pointed at the case. 'You can't carry that all the way across the Meadows.'

'I can.'

'I'll help you.'

They walked past the entrance to the Faculty of Music. A light was burning inside, in a high window; a practice room perhaps.

'If Nick said that he was seeing me later,' Jamie said, 'he didn't mean tonight. He meant some other time.'

Isabel affected nonchalance. 'Oh, I see.'

Jamie looked at her enquiringly. 'You don't like him, do you?'

She hesitated. 'I wouldn't choose him as a friend.'

'For me or for you? A friend for me or for you?'

She had to be careful. 'I wouldn't want to choose your friends for you. They're your business, not mine.'

He took a few moments to ponder this. 'Nick may not be easy,' he said. 'But I don't want to be unkind to him. And he's helping me with something.'

She waited for him to continue.

'You know I'm a hopeless composer,' he said. 'I've studied composition, of course. We all had to. But it's just not some-thing that I've ever really had a talent for. And so I asked him to help me with something that I'd been working on for months, but getting nowhere with. And he did. He's been knocking it into shape for me.'

She glanced at him. He was transferring the bassoon case from one hand to the other. 'Let me carry it just for a little while.'

He rejected her help with a shake of the head. 'It could be worse,' he said. 'It could be the contra.'

She felt relieved by what he had said about Nick, but her curiosity was still nagging away at her. She had once heard something that he had written, a small bassoon solo, and she had liked it. But it had had no end, and he had explained that he could not think of how to resolve it. 'There are rules for resolution,' he said. 'But they don't seem to be working.'

'What are you writing?' she asked. She tried to make the question sound casual.

Jamie sighed. 'I didn't want to tell you. But I think that since you appear to be . . . well, a little bit jealous, I suppose I should.'

'I'm not jealous.' It sounded unconvincing, and that, she decided, was because she was jealous. 'Well, I am, actually.'

He smiled. 'And do you know something? I'm glad that you're jealous. I'm glad that you resent my spending time with other people. It's nice to be . . . to be wanted like that.'

She was surprised. She had imagined that he would resent possessiveness on her part; instead, it seemed that he was flattered by it. She had misread everything – again. She had imagined that Nick Smart had some sort of appeal for him, but it was just Jamie's kindness, that was all. Then she had been so careful, all along, right from the beginning of their relationship, not to appear as if she wanted to monopolise him, and now he said that he rather liked the idea of her wanting him all to herself. One can be wrong, she thought. One can be wrong about so much.

'Anyway,' Jamie continued, 'I'm going to tell you. I've been working on a piece for you. An Isabel piece. For the second anniversary of our . . . our getting together. That's what.'

Jamie's resolve to carry the bassoon all the way back weakened at the edge of the Meadows, when they reached the point where the drive bisected the park. In the distance, the reassuring yellow light of a taxi wove its way towards them, and he made the decision; Isabel, who was herself tired, did not object.

Within five minutes they were back at the house and Jamie paid off the taxi while Isabel went to open the front door.

Grace was full of indignation. She had been watching a television programme in which the expenses claims of a random group of parliamentarians had been scrutinised. One claimed, quite within the rules, a substantial sum for the removal of algae from his garden pond. Another had employed a number of relatives, none of whom struck her as being particularly qualified for their jobs.

'Our money,' snapped Grace.

'I think the removal of algae sounds ridiculous,' Jamie said.

'Of course to admit to algae is something,' Isabel mused. 'I'm not sure that I'd actually admit to having algae.'

Jamie's face broke into a smile. It was a typical Isabel remark, and he found it very funny. He had no idea why it should be in the slightest bit amusing, but it was. Grace did not think so.

'It wasn't him that had the algae. It was his garden pond,' she said. 'But I don't see why the taxpayers should pay for that.'

The conversation switched to Charlie. He had been as good as gold. She had read him the story about the caterpillar that consumed everything in sight, and he appeared to have understood it. He had grabbed the book and torn one of the pages, but she had stuck it together again. Then he had gone to bed and went off to sleep without protest.

Isabel said goodbye to Grace at the front door and returned to the kitchen, where Jamie was standing in the middle of the floor, his arms stretched up, yawning. He lowered his arms and embraced her.

'I was having a stretch,' he said. And then, 'You're the most wonderful woman, you know.'

She felt his arms about her. He was lithe like a sapling; spare. He was everything she desired; so beautiful in this and every light; so tender.

He kissed her and ran his hand down her back.

'Upstairs,' she said.

He switched off the kitchen light and they moved, hand in hand, to the foot of the stairs. Then Charlie started to wail, the sound drifting down from upstairs, a piercing, insistent howl.

She looked at Jamie and began to laugh.

'As between the claims of passion on the one hand,' she said, 'and on the other the claims of a child's crying – which are we programmed to respond to first? Which is the most urgent?'

'Passion?' ventured Jamie, but not seriously.

'I'm afraid not,' said Isabel. Her answer was the one that any woman would give, but not, she thought, any man.

11

Of all the tasks involved in running the delicatessen, Isabel most enjoyed preparing Cat's Special Mixture. This was convenient, as Eddie disliked anything to do with fish – 'Why don't they close their eyes when they die?' he had said, in serious objection – and Cat's Special Mixture involved that fishiest of fish, anchovies. It was largely composed of olives, though: green olives that were pitted, chopped in half, and then mixed in colourful promiscuity with strips of red and yellow pepper. The whole was then marinated, with the anchovies, in extra-virgin olive oil, and the resulting mix was placed in a large bowl. It was not to everyone's taste – and certainly not to Eddie's – but Isabel enjoyed both making and eating it. And it helped her to think, she decided, sitting there with her hands covered in oil and the smell of anchovy in her nostrils.

It was now Wednesday, and she had three more days in the delicatessen, including Saturday, which was always extremely busy. Cat would be back late on Sunday and, feeling guilty, would insist on returning to work on Monday morning. She had already been in touch from Sri Lanka, having sent a message to Isabel telling her that the villa had exceeded her expectations and that she would not be coming back. That's a joke, she added, but yes, I could stay here for ever. Did you know, Isabel, that this country was called Serendip? I suppose you did, as you know so much. I didn't. But imagine living in Serendip.

Isabel wondered what would happen if Cat for some reason really did fail to return. Would she be landed with responsibility for the delicatessen, or would Eddie somehow rise to the occasion? Cat was adamant that he could not run the business by himself, but had anybody ever asked him? Even Isabel had assumed that he would be too anxious to manage by himself, but did these assumptions only serve to reinforce whatever anxieties he felt? She wondered whether it was not a bit like learning to swim: if one was expected to hang on, then one did; if one was expected to strike out by oneself, then that is what one did.

She thought of this as she pitted the olives. On Friday she had planned to meet Stella Moncrieff for lunch. She had not yet determined what she was going to say to her, but she had a day or two to decide on that. Travelling to and from lunch, and the lunch itself, would take about two hours out of her working day. She had no compunction in asking Eddie to run the shop single-handedly for that length of time, but if he could manage for a couple of hours, then why not make it the whole day? There were other things that she wanted to do on Friday, which was an important day for her. Edward Mendelson, Auden's literary executor, was delivering a lecture at the university in the late afternoon, and he was due to have dinner at the house after the reception that followed the lecture. Isabel had written to him on several occasions, and they had met briefly in Oxford, when he had been giving lectures at Christ Church and she had been at a conference of women philosophers at Somerville. Isabel had felt awkward about the meeting of women philosophers: would men have been allowed to convene a similarly exclusive meeting? She thought not. Nor were men allowed to have men's colleges any more, and yet Cambridge maintained three women-only colleges, even if Somerville had now decided to admit men.

If she took Friday off in its entirety, then she could spend the morning on the next issue of the *Review*, which always seemed to be due at the printer's sooner than she imagined, and then she could have lunch with Stella Moncrieff. Edward Mendelson's lecture was at four, and she could skip the reception in order to get back to the house to spend time with Charlie and to get the meal ready. Looked at in this way, Friday simply did not leave time to work at the delicatessen.

She beckoned Eddie over to the table where she was dealing with the olives. She discreetly closed the jar containing the anchovy fillets: even the smell of them could make Eddie nauseated, or so he claimed.

The young man looked at her quickly before his eyes slid away. It was like that with him; there would be a bit of progress, he would become more confident, and then suddenly he would regress, back to awkwardness and reserve. This time, she thought, the reason is that five hundred pounds; he thinks I am going to ask him about it.

'Eddie,' she said, 'I want to talk to you about Friday.'

His eyes still remained fixed on the floor.

'Look at me, Eddie,' she said, 'you should look at people when they talk to you.' I sound like a schoolmarm, she thought.

He raised his eyes, held her gaze for the briefest of moments, and then looked away again.

Isabel sighed. 'Friday. I'm going to be very busy this Friday.'

'It's always busy on Fridays,' said Eddie. 'Almost as bad as Saturday. Some people start their weekend on Friday, you see.'

His observation hardly made it easier for her. But she had made up her mind; and if Eddie could cope by himself on a Friday, then he should be able to cope at any time. She explained what she had in mind. 'You'll be all right,' she said. 'And you can have the number of my mobile phone. I'll switch it on just for you. If anything crops up and you need my advice, then just phone me.' She paused. 'Except during the lecture I'm going to.'

A flicker passed over his face – anxiety, she thought, doubt. But then he shrugged. 'All right. Will you be here on Saturday?'

'Of course. It's just Friday that's the problem. And thank you, Eddie.'

There was silence.

Isabel reached out and touched him on the forearm. 'Listen, that money, that five hundred pounds. It's a gift from me to you. I'm not thinking about it, but I can tell you are.'

He looked up at her now; his lower lip was trembling. 'I wasn't thinking about it.'

She did not want to contradict him; he was so vulnerable, so uncertain of himself. But if people always avoided engaging with him, then she wondered whether he would ever make any progress; some boils needed to be lanced. And so she said, quite gently, 'You were, Eddie. I think you were.'

He looked at her resentfully. 'I know what I'm thinking. What gives you the idea that you can tell me what I'm think-ing, when I'm not . . .' His words trailed away, and suddenly, without any warning, he began to sob. He reached down and

138

brought the bottom of his apron up to wipe at his eyes. She thought for a moment that he was going to blow his nose on it – and he obviously thought so too, as he hesitated, but did not.

He began to turn away, but she reached out and took hold of him. 'You told me that you were in trouble, and you obviously are. Why not tell me?'

He began to get control of his sobbing. 'I lied to you. I'm not in trouble. I lied to you to get the money.'

This took a moment to sink in. His anguish, it seemed, was caused not by some nameless bit of trouble into which he had got himself, but by his guilt over having lied to her. In a curious way this made Isabel feel relieved: she might not be able to sort out any trouble into which he had strayed, but she could grant him expiation of his guilt. She could forgive the deception; that would be easy – a matter of a few words.

'All right,' she said. 'You lied to me to get me to give you money. But now you've confessed. You've told me about it, and that means I can say that it doesn't matter, that I forgive you.' She watched him. His hands, which had been shaking, were still. He was listening very carefully, she could tell.

'And I really do forgive you. I mean what I say. It's all right.'

He looked up. 'You don't mind?'

'Don't mind? Of course I mind – or minded. Nobody likes to be lied to. Especially by somebody they know. Somebody they thought of as a friend. So I did mind . . . *did*. Not now. That's what forgiving somebody is all about. You say, I minded, but now it doesn't matter any more. It's rubbed out.'

'Well, I'm sorry I lied.'

She still held him, but she felt his arm move slightly; he

wanted to get away. He would have to learn about apology. 'So now you're apologising to me?'

'Yes. Sorry.'

She shook her head. 'That's not a full apology, Eddie. You can't just say sorry. You have to say something about why you did what you did. Then you say sorry.'

'I wanted the money.'

No, that would not do. 'Why?'

He did not speak for a while. A customer had entered the delicatessen and was peering at a display of dried pasta. Eddie watched him; he mistrusted customers until he knew them well; there were too many shoplifters, he said.

Isabel dropped her voice. 'We can still talk. Why did you need that five hundred pounds?'

Eddie turned to her. 'My father's got this hip, see. It's really painful. They can give him one of these new ones, you know those metal hips they put in. But they can't do it for a year. They say that there's . . .'

'A waiting list?'

'Yes.'

A year of pain. That was what socialised medicine meant; sometimes pain had to be endured if nobody was to go without the basics.

'So you wanted to get it done privately? To pay for it?'

He nodded, and she watched him closely. He did not look away; his eyes moved slightly, the normal flicker of movement that comes with consciousness, but he did not look away.

'Do you know how much it costs?' she asked. 'Do you know how much it costs to have it done at the Murrayfield Hospital? The surgeon's fees? The anaesthetist? The physiotherapy, and so on?'

Now he looked away. 'Five hundred,' he muttered. 'Something like that.'

'Oh, Eddie . . .' She was about to say that five hundred pounds was not very much, but she realised in time that that was exactly what she should not say. So she said instead, 'It's much more expensive than that.'

He said nothing. He was fiddling with the strings of his apron, twisting them round a finger. She watched him for a moment, and then made her decision. 'I can pay for this, you know. I can pay for the whole thing. I can do that for your father.'

Her words had an immediate effect. The twirling of the apron string stopped as Eddie froze. He did not move.

'Yes,' said Isabel. 'I can easily do it. You see, I have a special fund that allows me to do things like that. I give grants, or rather the lawyer gives them. We can do that very easily.'

'You can't pay for other people's operations,' said Eddie.

'Why not? If they need them. Why not?'

'Because it's their own business.' It was crudely put, but she knew exactly what he meant. In philosophical terms she would have referred to it as individual autonomy, or the sphere of private decision. But what Eddie had said summed it up very well.

'All right,' she said. 'I'll keep out of it. But if you change your mind, then I'll do it. You just let me know.'

She realised that she had said nothing about the return of the five hundred pounds. If that was not going to be anywhere near the sum required for the operation, then Eddie should surely offer to return it. Indeed, he *had* to return it. But he said nothing about it, and just turned away to get on with his work. And that was the point at which she realised that the whole business about the father's hip replacement was a complete lie.

It hurt her, being lied to by Eddie, and it made her reflect on

141

why exactly it was that we were harmed by lies. Sometimes, of course, lies harmed us because we acted on them, and this proved to be to our detriment. That was straightforward and under-standable. The person falsely directed on to the cliff path by the mischievous passerby is harmed by the lie when he falls over the edge. The fraudster's victim is harmed when he sends money for the non-existent benefit that will never materialise. He suffers loss. But what of other lies – lies which did not necessarily make us act to our disadvantage, nor took anything from us, but which just misled us? Why should we be hurt by them?

It is all because of trust, she decided. We trusted others to tell us the truth and were let down by their failure to do so. We were hoodwinked, shown to be credulous, which is all about loss of face. And then she decided that it was nothing to do with trust, or pride. It was something to do with the moral value of things as they really were. Truth was built into the world; it informed the laws of physics; truth *was* the world. And if we lied about something, we disrupted, destabilised that essential truth; a lie was wrong simply because it was *that which was not*. A lie was *contra naturam*. Truth was beauty, beauty truth. But was Keats right about that? If truth and beauty were one and the same thing, then why have two different terms to describe it? Ideas expressed in poetry could be beguiling, but philosophically misleading, even vacuous, like the rhetoric of politicians who uttered the most beautiful-sounding platitudes about scraps of dreams, scraps of ideas.

But by Friday she had stopped thinking about Eddie and the lies he had told her. Isabel had a way of protecting herself against the discomforts of the world: she could make a decision to put them out of her mind and then do precisely that; it was of limited effect – things denied have a habit of coming back eventually, but as a temporary expedient it was effective enough. So by Thursday, she and Eddie were perfectly easy with one another; he had stopped thinking about the five hundred pounds, and the lie, as had she. It was as if nothing had happened.

Friday morning was devoted to editorial tasks, as she had planned, but not before she had spent a couple of hours with Charlie down on the canal tow-path feeding the ducks. Charlie watched in fascination, pointing and squealing with delight as the ducks swam for the crumbs Isabel tossed in their direction. I'm casting bread upon the waters, she thought. And then? Such bread was meant to return tenfold, but that was the difference between a metaphor and life: metaphors did not work when acted out. In the world of metaphor, the bread returned; in the world of ducks, it was eaten.

They returned from the canal and Isabel handed Charlie over to Grace. This was one area where denial did not work: I am not giving him as much time as he deserves, she thought. He wants all my time, and I am not giving it to him. But I am simply a working mother, she told herself, no different from anybody who takes her child to a nursery while she goes off to the office or the shop, or wherever she works. I should not feel guilty. But she did.

Her standing in for Cat at the delicatessen meant that her *Review* work had piled up. And that, she thought, is no metaphor: the work indeed stood in piles on her desk. The next issue was almost ready to go off to the printer, but behind that there stood submissions for the issue after that, including Dove's paper. Of the two articles for the next issue that still required her final attention, Isabel disposed of one within minutes; a few tiny points, mostly of a typographical nature, were dealt with and given the tick in green ink that Isabel used to show that it was finally ready. Then there was a piece by an American philosopher on the ethics of using traditional recipes from indigenous people (for want of a better term, thought Isabel: we are all indigenous to somewhere. She had never discovered anybody who was not). We took from people when we used their recipes, she wrote; we took their knowledge. It was not quite theft, but it was a taking. Isabel stopped reading and looked out of the window. Yes, but we were imitative creatures; we copied one another all the time, and it would be difficult to control such copying. But then she thought: Our drugs. We stop people from copying our drugs, even if they're dying. That's one sort of recipe we definitely do not share.

She was so engrossed in her work that she did not notice that midday had crept up on her, and when the grandfather clock in the hall struck it brought her back from the world of traditional recipes and exploitation, of out-of-control trolley cars and moral dilemmas, and back into the present world of lunch appointments. She had arranged to meet Stella Moncrieff in Glass and Thompson, the café at the top of Dundas Street that she liked to frequent. It was on the other side of town for both her and Stella – Princes Street being the divider, every bit as effective as a swift-flowing river, that split the city in two – but she liked that part of town with its galleries and views of the Fife hills. There was a pure, northern light there, she thought, a light that brought with it a sense of being on the edge of something, on the edge of silences and the wide plains of the North Sea.

Stella was waiting for her when she arrived, sitting at the table in the window.

'I've already ordered,' she said. She looked anxious, as if she feared that lunch might run out.

144

Isabel glanced at the menu on the board above the counter and placed her order. Then she joined Stella. She thought: The wives suffer in a very particular way.

Stella smiled at her, but the smile was clearly an effort. 'I don't know this place. I don't get out much these days . . .' She checked herself.

'I can imagine,' said Isabel quickly. She did not think that Stella wanted to sound self-pitying, and it was true: she did understand. Wives did not join the angry ranks of denouncers; they stood by their erring husbands, braving the photographers, although it was not hard to picture the scene behind the scenes, the rows and recriminations, the tears.

'Can you?' asked Stella. 'Can you imagine it?'

'I think I can,' said Isabel. 'I can imagine what it's like, with people thinking that your husband—'

'Was responsible for somebody's death,' Stella interjected. 'Because that's what they think.'

'Memory is short,' said Isabel. 'Disgrace doesn't always last very long. I know people in this city who have been disgraced over one thing or another. They thought it would last for ever; it doesn't. The press moves on to its next victim. Predators don't hang around the old kill too long.'

Stella attended closely to what she said. As if my words are particularly wise, thought Isabel. And I am only uttering platitudes; the obvious.

'Have you managed to do anything?' asked Stella when Isabel finished speaking; it was as if she had rapidly weighed, and discarded, Isabel's reassurances.

'A little,' said Isabel. 'I had lunch with your husband's assistant, Dr Brown. Norrie.'

Stella's eyes flickered, just briefly. 'I haven't seen him for some time,' she said. 'He's Marcus's nephew. His mother was Marcus's sister. Diana Moncrieff.'

'He told me that,' said Isabel.

Stella looked at Isabel expectantly. 'And what else did he say?'

The waiter brought two plates over to the table – Isabel's mozzarella and tomato salad and Stella's quiche. He put them down in front of them and asked if everything was all right. Isabel nodded, and he left.

Isabel drizzled olive oil over the tomatoes. Little islands of pesto floated in the clear pools of the oil; she saw the slices of mozzarella, domed, as tiny snow-covered mountains behind these islands. When you look closely at the small details, she thought, the world is different, more complex.

She had decided that she would tell Stella exactly what she had learned from Norrie Brown. She had no alternative really, as she could hardly lie to her and even if it would be hard for her to hear that her husband had deliberately falsified results, it might be better, in the long run, for her to confront this uncomfortable fact. People learned things like that about their spouses, and then forgave them. In a way it was easier; such knowledge could remove the sense of injustice that would otherwise linger, eating away at one's peace of mind. At least Stella would know the worst, could look it in the face, and then get on with life.

'This isn't very easy for me,' Isabel began.

Stella put down her fork and stared across the table. Isabel noticed that there were small lines radiating out from the corners of Stella's eyes, and that tiny fragments of make-up, flesh-coloured powder, had lodged in these little crevasses. The observation seemed to underline the humanity of the woman before her: we all put our best face to the world, comb our hair, tidy ourselves up; we all do that, because we want others to like us, to approve of how we look. And yet, at the heart of it was, in this case, a blot of shame, like a mark on the forehead: the wife of that doctor who killed that other man because he cut corners.

'What isn't easy for you?' Stella asked. She looked at Isabel reproachfully. 'Having lunch with me?'

'No. No. Not that. It's what I have to say that isn't particularly easy.'

For a few moments, Stella was silent. Then she said, 'You found something out?'

Isabel looked down at her plate. The other woman would want to know the opposite of what she was about to tell her. 'Yes, I'm sorry. I learned something from him.'

She related what Norrie had told her. Stella listened intently, with only slight signs of emotion – a reddening of her complexion, a movement of the mouth – when Isabel revealed the accusation of deliberate wrongdoing. Then, when Isabel had finished, they both sat quietly while Stella digested what had been said.

'So,' said Isabel. 'So what he suggested is that we leave well enough alone. And he's probably right, don't you think? Leave well enough alone. Your husband has been sufficiently punished: he's lost his job; it's the end of his career. Surely nobody would want him to suffer more than he has already.'

The control which Stella had shown now evaporated. She leaned forward across the table; her face flushed again, more angrily. 'And you believed him? You believed what Norrie told you? That nonsense? How can you be so naive?'

It took Isabel a moment to deal with the insult and to

recover her composure. But by then Stella had recanted. 'I'm sorry,' she said. 'I didn't mean to say that. I'm sure that you're not naive.' She paused; this was to be an apology, not a retraction. 'But I still don't think that you should have believed him.'

Isabel replied that she did not see any reason to disbelieve Norrie. People may lie when accused of wrongdoing, but the junior doctor had never been in the firing line. And what reason would he have to lie about a matter which had already been put to rest?

Stella listened, but started to shake her head vigorously before Isabel had finished speaking. 'But you don't know the background. You don't see how it all fits together.'

'I'm sorry,' said Isabel. 'You've lost me.'

Stella took a deep breath. 'Norrie Brown's mother, Diana Moncrieff, was a very difficult woman. She and Marcus had a great-aunt, Maggie, up in Inverness, an extremely wealthy woman who had a large farm on the Black Isle, a lovely place. Marcus and his sister used to go up there during school holidays every year. Maggie was childless and there was an understanding – which everybody spoke about quite openly – that she would leave the farm to Marcus and Diana jointly, and that it would not be split up but would be a sort of family base for both of them. That was very clearly understood, and Maggie herself talked about it. But when the old girl died, they found that she had not done this at all, but had left it to Marcus. It transpired that she had taken against Diana's husband for some reason or other. I have my theories. He was an Irishman, and they differed about Ulster. Maggie had some uncle on her mother's side who had been a relative of Carson's and was an ardent loyalist. She thought of Ulstermen as stranded Scots. These things last generations in Ireland.'

148

Isabel listened. There were issues like this in virtually every family, even if the stakes were rarely quite so high. It could be something quite small: a photograph, a keepsake, a small amount of money.

'Diana was devastated,' Stella continued. 'She confronted Marcus at the funeral, at the wake afterwards, one of those Highland affairs with lots of whisky and formal black suits. She told him that she expected him to keep to the understanding and share the farm with her. Marcus said no. He's not a greedy man, but it was the way she laid into him that made him dig in. He thought that had she asked politely, then he would probably have agreed. But he was not going to be dictated to like that. And after that, they never spoke again, directly that is.

'Then Diana died. She was killed in a car crash driving down from Inverness, just near Dalwhinnie. It's a lethal road that – it always has been. Marcus felt very bad about the row between him and Diana, and he tried to make it up to Norrie. When Norrie decided to do medicine, Marcus did what he could for him, including taking him under his wing. But I always suspected that Norrie resented him. I was convinced that Diana had poisoned him against Marcus, had spun him nonsense about being cheated out of the farm, and so on. I always thought that was there. Feelings of resentment like that never really go away, do they? They linger on.'

Yes, thought Isabel, and she reflected on her own family, where Cat had entertained feelings of intense jealousy over Jamie, forgiven her, patched it up, and then relapsed. Those feelings were always there, she thought, in spite of our best efforts to dispel them. Resentment lingers: it sounded like the name of a racehorse – not a successful one of course, racehorses should not linger unduly.

'You're smiling?'

She could not help herself; it is a concomitant of my allowing my thoughts to wander excessively, she thought. Then I smile or even say something. 'I'm sorry. It's nothing to do with what you've told me. It was just an odd thought about something else – about a racehorse . . .'

Stella stared at her intently. 'A racehorse?'

'Nothing,' said Isabel. 'It really has nothing to do with what we were talking about. Sometimes my mind wanders off. I'm sorry; you now have my full attention.'

Stella was silent, staring out of the window, out past Isabel, who was seated with her back to the street. Then, quite suddenly, her gaze shifted back to Isabel. 'Yes,' she said. 'Yes. That must be it. Norrie.'

Isabel looked at her expectantly.

'Norrie,' Stella went on, her tone becoming more forceful. 'What a perfect way of getting back at us. Perfect.'

Isabel understood. However, she could not help but sound incredulous; real life simply did not involve plots like that; real life was disappointingly mundane. 'Revenge? Do you really think so? Do you think that he – any doctor – would do that sort of thing? Risk people's lives?'

'Doctors do odd things,' snapped Stella. 'They're exactly the same as the rest of us.'

Isabel wrestled with the possibility. Stella was right about the frailty of doctors; they had extra-marital affairs, cheated on their tax returns, involved themselves in dirty politics. And there were spectacularly wicked doctors – doctors like Mengele – to show that for some the Hippocratic oath meant nothing. Anything was possible – from anyone. 'You're suggesting that Norrie altered the data? You're suggesting that he

150

did this to ruin Marcus? To ruin his uncle over some long-running sense of being deprived of something that his mother thought should be his?'

Stella's answer was simple. 'Yes. Exactly.'

Isabel, looking away from Stella, gazed out of the window. A man was walking up Dundas Street; a man wearing a chocolate-brown corduroy jacket of the fusty, vaguely raffish sort once worn by art teachers. He stopped and patted the pockets of his jacket, as if feeling for something that he hoped he had brought with him, before glancing in through the café window. His eyes met Isabel's, and he seemed to hesitate. There was recognition, but no recognition. We have met one another before, thought Isabel, and we both understand that. But we do not know who the other is, which speaks eloquently, she thought, of the way we live now, knowing more and more, but less and less.

12

Isabel felt relieved when Stella looked at her watch and announced that she had to leave. She suspected that it had been a trying meeting for both of them. For her part, she had been landed with the awkward task of telling Stella that Marcus had done precisely what he had been accused of doing; not an easy message for the wife of any wrongdoer to absorb. And then she had been obliged to listen to Stella labouring the point over Norrie Brown's grudge; the family feuds of others are never anything but discomforting for the rest of us. And Stella had been tenacious, worrying away at the ancient casus belli: Of course that's what he would have done. It would be the perfect revenge, don't you think?

Isabel had disagreed: People don't do that sort of thing. They just don't. And why do you think he would have shared his mother's feelings over the farm? He hardly ever went there – you told me that yourself. It wasn't a case of blue remembered hills. It would have been old business for him. But it seemed as if Stella heard none of this, or, if she heard it, dismissed it.

'What do you want me to do?' she had asked, when Stella looked at her watch. And she knew, even as she uttered the words, that they were the wrong ones. She should bow out of this now; she had done what she could to throw some light on the situation, and the light had turned to murk, complicated by the unlikely suggestion that Marcus's disgrace had all been engineered by an embittered nephew.

Stella did not wait to answer. 'Well, obviously I want you to . . . I'd like you, rather, to sort this out. If you wouldn't mind . . . I know I'm imposing on you.'

And she started to cry, the sobs coming up from somewhere within her, racking her frame. She struggled to control herself. 'I'm so sorry,' she said. 'I'm so sorry . . .'

Isabel leaned forward and put an arm around Stella's shoulder. At a neighbouring table a young man looked at them, and then looked away tactfully.

'You don't need to say you're sorry for being human,' whispered Isabel. 'Nobody needs to say sorry for that.'

'It's just that I've got nobody to help me,' said Stella. 'And so I latch on to you. And you were so kind to me. Said yes. I couldn't believe it . . . that somebody would help me out of the goodness of her heart.'

Now there was no possibility that Isabel could refuse. And as Stella calmed down, Isabel reassured her that she would not abandon the case. She heard herself say that – *the case* – and thought: Who do you think you are? You're beginning to talk like some ridiculous sleuth, when you're just Isabel Dalhousie, *intermeddler*. That was the right word, although it was heavy with self-criticism. She imagined the dictionary definition – intermeddler: one who meddles in affairs that are no business of hers; as in: 'Isabel Dalhousie was a real intermeddler' or 'Isabel Dalhousie, an *echt* intermeddler' (for *echt*, see the Real McCoy).

She stopped that line of thought, which could quickly lead

to an inappropriate, badly timed smile. *We do not smile when people weep / But weep we may / When people smile.* The lines came from nowhere, as such lines did to her; unbidden, but redolent of something elusive, only half-understood – sometimes – and oddly memorable, as had been those lines about the tattooed man that she had whispered to Jamie before they fell asleep together in each other's arms; the tattooed man who had loved his wife and was proud of his son, the tattooed baby. They were ridiculous, and frequently trite, but these little stories, these little snatches of poetry, provided their modicum of comfort, their islands of meaning that we all needed to keep the nothingness at bay; or at least Isabel felt that she needed them.

'I'll do what I can.'

She meant to sound businesslike, and she did. But she also sounded cold, she thought; which was misleading, because she did not begrudge the other woman her help. Have the courage of your convictions, she thought. So what if you're an intermeddler? Intermeddle, and don't feel bad about it. And there was a possibility, just a possibility, that Stella was right. Isabel had not liked Norrie Brown, although she had been unable to decide why this should be so. Now the doubts began to implant themselves in her mind. She did not like Norrie Brown because he was a liar. Isabel had always been able to sense lies; it was a sixth sense – a sixth sense that nosed out mendacity, and it had warned her about Norrie Brown. She had not been listening at the time, and had not picked up the warning. But now it seemed to her that it was coming through clearly, a strong signal from the utterly inexplicable intuitive headquarters that women had and which men, she suspected, might just miss out on. But that was another issue; something for a special edition of the *Review* which would engage the feminist philosophers, the advocates of the philosophy of care. Yes, they would love it, as they relished any chance to put men in their place. 'Female Intuition as a Resource in Moral Philosophy' would be a good title for the issue, and it would attract scores of submissions. But no, she would not do that, because she did not like some of the feminist philosophers; ideologues, she thought, and strident, too. And yet, and yet . . . There was Christopher Dove, for example, and his friend Professor Lettuce. Had it ever entered their heads that their perspective on the world was a specifically male one, and not the view from nowhere? They had both condescended to her in a way in which they would not condescend to a man; they needed to be taught a lesson. They *needed* feminism.

She turned to Stella and saw her, suddenly, in a new light. Here was a woman who felt powerless. The might of the male-dominated medical councils had been directed against her husband. A pack of journalists – probably all male, at least in the case of those who would have led the pack – had crucified him. And she could do nothing about it, but watch despair engulf him, and shed her tears, as she had just done, in full public view.

Isabel had already made her decision, but now it became even firmer. 'Yes,' she said. 'I'll look into your theory about Norrie.'

Stella thanked her. 'Except it's not just a theory,' she said. 'I think that it's true. I really do. And I think that you'll find the same thing.'

Edward Mendelson's lecture was not until four, which was a good two hours away. As she said goodbye to Stella outside

Glass and Thompson, Isabel wondered what to do with those two hours. If she walked home, she would have half an hour, at the most, to spend with Charlie before she had to leave again for the lecture. If she took a bus, it would not be much different: the traffic was heavy, and there were road works in Hanover Street that were holding everything up. The answer, then, was to stay in town for the next hour and then make her way up to George Square, where the lecture was being held.

It was only a short distance down Dundas Street to the Scottish Gallery, and Isabel sauntered in that direction, glancing on the way into the windows of the neighbouring galleries. One of them, which specialised in sporting scenes and landscapes, displayed a large china hare, caught in mid-leap, astonishingly realistic. And just behind him, beneath a large display easel, lurked a porcelain fox, almost life-size, his coat sleek with glaze, his eyes looking out on to the street, bright and wary with the cunning of his species. Brother Fox. She stopped and looked at him; he was so naturally rendered that were he to be placed in her garden, half-hidden, perhaps, by a shrub, he would be indistinguishable from Brother Fox himself. But Brother Fox would not be fooled because he simply would not see him; without a smell, he would not see him – the smell gave everything away. She smiled: it was the same with liars.

The Scottish Gallery was mounting an exhibition of paintings by exiled Polish artists who had made their home in Scotland. There were not many of them, but they had painted enough to cover the walls, and were being examined by a group of five or six visitors. Isabel heard a snatch of Polish, or what she assumed was Polish, and she saw one of the group, a young woman in jeans, turn to a man and point at the label below one of the paintings. He leaned forward and exclaimed enthusiastically, and called to the others who had moved on to another painting.

A voice behind her whispered, 'They keep finding something. Scraps of their history. It's a very emotional exhibition for Poles.'

She turned to find Robin McClure, one of the gallery's directors, standing behind her. 'I suppose there's such a big gap for them,' she said. 'How many years? Forty years of ice.'

'Well, they carried on painting. Or some did.'

Isabel stared at one of the paintings: a girl in a room looking out of a window; a feeling of desolation. And beside it a grey landscape under a grey sky – was that Poland? The closest she had been to Poland was Berlin, where already one had the sense of plains stretching out into a sorrowful emptiness further east; and now here it was in paint, greyness and sorrow.

'I'm becoming depressed,' she said, her voice lowered; she did not want the Poles to hear her say that their landscape, or their paintings, depressed her.

'I was just about to make myself a pot of tea,' said Robin. 'It's warm enough to sit outside. We've got a little table out the back.'

She followed him down the stairs, past the display cases, and into the small garden. The table stood on a patch of raked white gravel, two French ironwork chairs on either side. Isabel sat in one of these while Robin went back to fetch the tea; she closed her eyes and let the sun play on her face. There was a bird singing in a tree somewhere over the wall that divided the ground at the rear of the building into patches of urban garden. Geraniums were in blossom somewhere close by; she could smell them, that sweet, velvety odour. She opened her eyes and saw that there was a tub of the flowers not far away; red clusters against dark green leaves. The smell took her back, to some-where far away and long ago; somewhere she could not quite remember . . . and then she thought: Georgetown, and her window box. There had been geraniums in the window box, planted by the previous tenant, who, like her, had been a research fellow in philosophy, and had confessed that the gera-niums were the only things she had ever planted in her life. 'All I leave behind me,' she had said, 'are some gerania,' and laughed.

Robin returned with a generously sized teapot and a couple of mugs. Tucked under his arm was a glossy auction catalogue, which he retrieved once he had put down the mugs. 'Sotheby's,' he said, nodding in the direction of the catalogue. 'Just in. Their next sale of old masters.'

She reached up for the catalogue and looked at the front cover, much of which was taken up with a picture of a small family group huddled under an oak tree. '"*Rest on the Flight into Egypt*,"' she read. '"Jan Brueghel, the Elder."'

'But not the oldest,' said Robin, looking over her shoulder. 'One of the dynasty. Son of Pieter and father of Jan the Younger. There was quite a clan of them.'

Isabel scrutinised the painting. 'Not much seems to be hap-pening,' she said.

'Well, they are resting.'

'Of course.'

'And the whole point of the painting is the oak tree,' Robin went on. 'The flight into Egypt is pretty much incidental.'

He began to pour the tea. 'But things happen in some Brueghels. Do you know that famous Bruegel – Pieter Bruegel, that is – *The Massacre of the Innocents*? It's one of the busiest old masters around. There's an awful lot going on. I saw it the other day, as it happens. There was an exhibition of Flemish paintings and it was in it.'

Isabel thought. 'No. I don't think so. Which innocents were they?'

'Dutch innocents,' said Robin, passing her a mug of tea. 'Dutch innocents – massacred by Spanish troops. Except . . .'

'Except?'

'Except the painting – or one version of it – tells a different story. A later owner found it too vivid and ordered the truth to be painted over.'

'That wouldn't have been the first time that a painting was changed in that way,' said Isabel. 'Nor the last, for that matter. I was in a gallery in Moscow once and saw a picture of the Politburo with the non-persons painted out.'

Robin smiled. 'Probably more successfully than the Bruegel. The problem with *The Massacre of the Innocents* is that you look at it and you wonder why the soldiers are all stabbing a very large turkey. And why is a large bag of wheat lying on the ground, in the middle of nowhere? Then you see the children underneath the turkey and the sack, painted over, but no longer well concealed. A restorer has made a start and then maybe not liked what he saw underneath.'

Isabel paged through the catalogue. The old masters revealed the small range of their interests – or those of their patrons. Endless religious scenes, low-country landscapes, the occasional interior. 'I wish they'd been free to paint other things,' she said. 'More reportage. More work scenes. More life as it was.'

Robin sipped at his tea. 'Painters rarely paint for posterity. They portray the things that people want to admire at the time.'

Isabel frowned. She was not sure that she agreed. '*Guernica*?'

Robin put down his mug. 'Yes, I suppose so. I suppose

Picasso wanted to put that on the record.' He paused. The bird in the neighbouring tree had raised the pitch of his song, and for a few moments they both listened to the ringing challenge. Then Robin rose to his feet. 'I almost forgot. That painting.'

Isabel looked up from the catalogue. 'What painting?'

Robin was making his way back into the gallery. 'Hang on a sec. I'll get it,' he said over his shoulder.

Isabel turned a page of the catalogue. A worldly wise infant looked out from his mother's knee; above his head, a thin circle of gold, a halo; in the background, a line of cypresses marched off across a landscape that was Tuscany or Umbria. She looked at the mother's face, at the expression of gentle solemnity that seemed to be the approved look of motherhood. Had she ever looked at Charlie quite like that?

Robin reappeared, carrying a small painting, a double hand-breadth or so across, which he put down on the table in front of Isabel. 'Here it is,' he said. 'It came back from the framer yesterday.'

She gave a start. It was another fox; a small painting of a fox, standing in a clearing, sniffing the air.

'Brother Fox,' she muttered.

Robin sat down again and reached for the teapot. 'Brother who?'

She picked up the painting and looked for a signature.

'Nothing,' said Róbin. 'No clue as to the artist. But rather well executed. A nice little painting.'

Isabel put the painting back on the table. 'Yes,' she said. 'It's nice. But . . . but why are you showing it to me?'

Robin looked puzzled. 'Jamie said that you'd collect it. He bought it a few weeks ago and said that you'd be in for it.'

'My Jamie?'

'Yes.'

She was at a loss as to what to say. Robin, watching her, looked puzzled. 'Is there something wrong with the frame? We thought it was rather a good choice.'

'No. The frame's fine.' Isabel looked at the painting again. The only conclusion she could reach was that Jamie had bought it for her as a present. But then why would he not have told her to go in and collect it, if that was what he had wanted? He had forgotten; that must be it. The important thing was that Jamie had bought it for her. He had come in and bought it for her. 'He'll probably be in for it himself,' she said. 'I won't take it now.'

She closed her eyes for a few moments, feeling again the sun on her brow. The moment was delicious, one to be savoured. I shall remember this, she thought. The painting would not have been cheap, and he would have paid for it with his hard-earned money. How many music lessons did a small painting of a fox represent? Twenty? Thirty? No matter: Jamie had specially chosen it for her, and that showed that he loved her, which is what she wanted to know, more than anything else. It was a moment of realisation, of understanding, and it took place against a background of sun and geraniums and the pure voice of a bird.

13

She still felt elated when she sat down for the lecture in the George Square Lecture Theatre. So a child might feel on Christmas Eve, she thought – filled with anticipation for the gifts to come. But she did not analyse her sense of pleasure beyond that, and it was as well, perhaps, as Jamie had not given her a present before, if one did not count birthday and Christmas presents, which were reciprocal, anyway. The painting of a fox was a perfect choice; Brother Fox was their secret, the one that she shared with him. Grace saw him, of course, but did not like him, and in particular believed that he was slowly destroying the garden.

'There'll be nothing left by the time he's finished,' she had complained, after Brother Fox had succeeded in unearthing a cluster of bulbs that had been carefully planted the year before. Now they lay exposed, one gnawed slightly and then spat out, the others tossed carelessly about the edge of the lawn.

'Vandal,' Grace continued. 'You know that man who came to deal with the wasps last year? That man from somewhere out near Peebles? Well, he told me that he knows how to deal with urban foxes. He traps them and then takes them out into the country and lets them loose.'

'That's what he says he does,' Isabel retorted.

Grace met the challenge with a stare. 'Yes. That's what he does.'

'But I suspect that he doesn't,' said Isabel. 'He just says that so that the urbanites feel all right about it. Dalkeith is very different from Edinburgh. They're not particularly sentimental out there. He'll kill them. And he can do it. Foxes are officially vermin.'

Grace said nothing, but pointedly picked up the bulbs and began to replant them.

'He has to live,' muttered Isabel, and left her to it.

'And so do bulbs,' said Grace.

Isabel almost said, 'It's my garden, and if I want to let the fox dig things up, then that's my affair.' But she did not. She could have said it, since it was true, and it was perfectly reasonable that one should allow a fox free rein of one's garden if one liked foxes, which she did. But she had never asserted her rights as employer and owner, and never would. Grace was treated as a colleague; requests to do things were never given as orders, and most of all Isabel never acted as if her money gave her power. It did – and she knew it – but she never abused it. Yet there were limits, which both understood. Grace could not call the man from Dalkeith to deal with Brother Fox because the garden was not hers; both understood that.

Now, sitting in the second row of the lecture theatre, she put the fox painting out of her mind and looked about her. Edward Mendelson's lecture had been widely publicised by the Scottish Poetry Library and by the *Scotsman*, with the result that several hundred people had bought tickets, and even if the lecture theatre would not be full, it would not look empty. She felt relieved; she had been to enough philosophy lectures where a small turn-out had brought embarrassment to both speakers and hosts. In Cambridge there had been a professor who had always said the same thing on such occasions, even on fine days: *This weather keeps people in* and *It's so hard for people these days.* That had been greeted with nods of understanding, but she had always wondered why it was so hard for people these days. Was it any harder to attend a philosophy lecture than it had ever been? Surely not; if anything, it would be easier. Lecture theatres in the past had always been uncomfortable, perhaps deliberately so, in order to keep the audience attentive. The old anatomy lecture theatre in the university was famous for its discomfort; narrow, knee-bending benches ranged steeply, almost vertiginously upwards – the better to allow a view, of course, of the dissection below, but hardly comfortable. And other lecture theatres had been little better; no soft seats, cold, noisy in the wrong way; everything that the modern lecture theatre or seminar room now eschewed. No, it was not hard for people these days, or rather, if life was still hard, then it was less hard than it had ever been before.

She looked up at the ceiling. Who had said *You've never had it so good*? Harold Macmillan, a long time ago – and he had been addressing the electorate. Politicians did not speak like that to the electorate these days. They might well say *I know how hard it is for people these days*, and people would like that, because they did feel that it was hard. And for some, many indeed, it was.

There was a programme, which she now studied in the lecture theatre's dim light. Edward Mendelson, it announced, is the literary executor of W. H. Auden and the Lionel Trilling

164

Professor in the Humanities at Columbia University. He is the author of numerous critical works on Auden, and is editing the poet's *Complete Works*. His subject tonight is guilt, neurosis, and the elucidation of a moral standpoint.

Guilt, thought Isabel, and found herself wondering what Marcus Moncrieff would be doing now – while she was sitting in this lecture theatre, he would be slumped in his armchair, she imagined, just as he had been when she visited their flat; sitting and staring out over the top of Princes Street to the hills of Fife beyond. He's innocent, she thought. He's an innocent man wrongly condemned to shame and the end of the career that had been his life.

Of course, there were other innocent men suffering for things they did not do. Isabel wondered what proportion of those in prison were innocent of the crimes of which they had been convicted. She had read somewhere that the figure for this was between five and ten per cent, which meant that at least one in twenty of those in prison had simply not done what they were accused of doing. And in places where they executed people, then presumably some at least of those who faced death did so as innocent people. Did those who signed the death warrants or turned down the last-minute appeals for clemency ever think, *This might be an innocent man?*

She could not help the innocent in prison, but she could help a man who had been otherwise unjustly punished. Or, rather, she could try.

Edward Mendelson delivered his lecture. Auden, he said, had a strong sense of guilt, which was neurotic in origin. There was plenty of evidence for that in the poems, but should we concern ourselves with the roots of the poet's engagement with morality, or should we look rather at what the great artist has done to transform his personal neuroses into a vision of moral truth that we all can share? He put the question, and Isabel, from the second row, made her own choice without having to think about it very much. The work of art was what mattered to her – the moral statement that helped us to live better, which is what, she believed, the purpose of art was. She was not interested in the doubts and infirmities that preceded the lines that minted a truth: it was the lines themselves that mattered, and we should not diminish their force by diminishing the poet. Auden behaved badly on occasion, as we all did. He lived in domestic squalor, his personal conversation could be arch, he worshipped punctuality, he became irritable. But none of that diminished the truth of what he said. And there were other writers whose personal lives did not bear examination. At least Auden managed money sensibly. Writers – and musicians – generally handled money badly.

She slipped out at the end of the lecture. A well-known Edinburgh bore, famous for his buttonholing of distinguished visitors, had positioned himself at the foot of the steps that led down from the stage. There would be no escape for Edward Mendelson now unless the organisers of the lecture were prepared to be ruthless and sweep their guest past the bore; push him over, perhaps. She glanced over her shoulder as she left the theatre: a phalanx had assembled around the lecturer and somebody was gesturing for him to accompany them, but the bore was on to them, and like a rugby forward he nimbly dodged past the literary editor of the *Scotsman*, wove past the professor of English literature, and positioned himself in front of Edward Mendelson. 'Professor Mendelson, something you said rather interested me . . .'

Isabel walked out of the lecture theatre bemused. The bore was an earnest man who believed in a civilised society of conversation and debate, an Edinburgh of the Scottish Enlightenment; but such an Edinburgh would always exclude those who tried too hard. So he had become a lonely man, accustomed to the glassy looks of others; she should make more effort with him, she thought, because all of us should take on our allocation of lame ducks. But the last time she had seen him, at the opening of a special exhibition at the Royal Scottish Museum, he had addressed her on the subject of wind farms, and as he spoke she had suddenly formed a mental image of the bore talking endlessly at high volume, while before him spun round the blades of a small power-generating windmill, driven by the hot air.

She detached herself from the crowd milling round the entrance to the lecture theatre and made her way out into George Square. It was not yet Festival time, but a small group of men was already erecting the Spiegeltent in the gardens of the square; later there would be marquees, crowds and per-formers, talented and otherwise. She walked along the cobbled lane in front of the university library; a student, engaged in conversation on a mobile phone, gestured to emphasise his point. He was angry, thought Isabel, and wondered what the cause of his anger was. Betrayal? Infidelity? The selfishness of a flatmate? She wanted to say to him: Does it really matter? But it did matter, of course, as these small things do.

She walked on and became aware that somebody was walk-ing immediately behind her. She slowed down, and the person behind her drew abreast. She glanced sideways: Nick Smart.

His manner was casual. 'I saw you at the lecture,' he said. 'I was surprised.'

She looked at him quickly, but did not keep eye contact. It

annoyed her that he should be surprised to see her at the lecture; Auden was her poet, and this was her city. Why should he be surprised? Was it because he thought that she was somehow unworthy of Auden?

'I wouldn't have thought he was your sort of poet,' Nick went on.

Isabel stopped. She turned to face him. 'Why do you say that?' she demanded. She felt hot – and angry.

Nick shrugged. 'Just not your sort.'

She suddenly thought: He's laying claim to him, and I'm excluded.

'What sort of poet would you expect me to like?' she asked, and then, 'I find that sort of assumption rather irritating . . .'

Her reply did not seem to disturb him. That smug expression, she thought; that demeanour of condescension. But then his expression changed. 'I'm sorry,' he said. 'I didn't mean to offend you.'

She started to walk again, and he continued with her; they were stuck with one another at least until the end of the lane, unless one of them were to turn and walk back.

'Don't think about it,' she said. 'It's all right.'

'You've taken against me,' said Nick. 'I don't know what I've done, but you've taken against me.'

'I don't know why you think that,' said Isabel. Of course I have, she thought, but how can one confess pure dislike – to the object of the dislike?

Nick shook his head. 'Maybe I'm imagining it.'

'Maybe.'

They had reached the end of the lane, and Isabel began to bear left, towards the Meadows. 'I hope that you enjoyed the lecture,' she said.

Nick mumbled something that she did not hear, and moved off in the opposite direction. She watched him for a moment and felt, almost immediately, a strong sense of regret. Nick Smart was an unhappy man – that was apparent. He was, she imagined, lonely; living in a strange city where he had no past, no links, could not be easy. And she had allowed a visceral dislike to overcome her sense of what she should do, which was to forgive him his condescension, his egregious elegance, and at least say something kind to him, which she had not done. She stopped and turned round. He was walking up one side of George Square, along the edge of the gardens in the centre. He was looking at the ground, his head bowed.

Isabel hesitated. It was wrong, she knew, quite wrong, to allow gratuitous bad feeling to exist between oneself and another. She should run after him; she should apologise; she should try to restore courteous relations between them. She stood still; by now Nick Smart was almost at the top of the square, and in a few moments he walked off to the right and disappeared. It would have been easy, but now it was too late – taking a few steps to apologise was one thing, running after somebody was another, or seemed to be another; it was as if by turning the corner he had walked out of the circle of her moral concern. She turned away and began to walk home. It was as good an illustration as any, she thought, of the proposition that we forget about those who are distant from us, whom we cannot see – the starving in some far-off land, the oppressed whose suffering is known only by vague report, the man who has walked round a corner. I have broken relations with him, she said to herself, and as she thought this she was reminded of a curious habit she had had as a young girl. If ever she said something uncharitable to another, she would ask herself, What if that person died right now? How would I feel?

169

The childish trick worked in exactly the way it always did. She felt guilty; she regretted her lack of charity. Nick Smart was a stranger, far from home, and she had not comforted him.

'But why should I?' she asked herself.

'Because he is your moral neighbour,' a voice within her said. 'Because you came into contact with him; that was all. But it was enough to make you behave towards him with decency, which you did not do because you are jealous and possessive.'

The branches of the trees moved gently, nudged by a wind that Isabel barely felt.

'Am I?' she asked the voice.

'Oh yes,' it replied. 'Very.'

Conscience, she thought, walks with us; an unobtrusive companion, unseen, perhaps, but still audible.

Later, having been released from the post-lecture reception, Edward Mendelson made his way up to Isabel's house for dinner. Jamie was busy putting Charlie to bed when he arrived, and so Isabel entertained him herself in the ground floor draw-ing room.

'It's just us,' she explained. 'You said that you didn't want me to have a large dinner party. So it's just Jamie, you and me.'

'Exactly what I wanted,' he said. And then, 'Jamie . . . I don't believe that I've met him.'

'You haven't,' said Isabel. 'When were you last in Edinburgh? Five years ago?'

'About that. He's . . .' The question went unfinished.

'My boyfriend,' said Isabel. 'Actually a bit more than that. We have a child together. A little boy.'

Edward Mendelson inclined his head in congratulation. 'I'm delighted.'

Isabel poured them both a glass of wine, and for the next few minutes they discussed the lecture. Then Jamie appeared. He looked happy, thought Isabel; relaxed and happy. Charlie, it seemed, had that effect on him; and perhaps Charlie would grow up to be one of those people who made others happy just to be in his company. And would Charlie look like Jamie, she wondered, or be a male version of me? That one could not imagine, she decided; none of us could see ourselves as the opposite sex. Of course he might look like neither, as children often did; confounding recent genes in favour of ancient ones.

The conversation flowed easily. Jamie asked about a production at the Met that he had read about in the papers; Edward Mendelson had seen it, and thought highly of it.

'Auden had to live near a good opera house, didn't he?' said Isabel.

'Yes, which is why Kirchstetten suited him. It's only forty miles or so from Vienna.'

Isabel was silent. She knew that Edward Mendelson had been at the funeral in Kirchstetten; that he had been there when they played Siegfried's Funeral March on a gramophone and then carried the poet from his house and the local brass band had struck up and accompanied the cortège through the streets of the village that had been so proud of the Herr Professor. She wanted to ask, what was it like? but could not, because it was not a question that could be answered easily. Sad, of course. Tearful, surely. But in her mind there must have been a poignancy that transcended normal grief; as there must have been at that other Austrian funeral, in the rain, when Mozart was laid in his pauper's grave; the death of poetry, the death of music, which leaves us nothing if those two things should die.

They talked again about the lecture.

'Just where is the line between a rational sense of guilt,' Isabel asked, 'and a neurotic one?'

'In a difficult place, I expect,' said Edward Mendelson. 'These lines are often fine.'

'But you can tell when somebody's crossed that line,' said Jamie.

Isabel was interested. She was thinking of Marcus. There was no reason for him to feel guilty, if Stella's view was correct, and yet he felt shame – that was obvious enough. So that was a case of shame following upon guilt which other people thought should be there, but which was not. You cannot feel guilty about a wrong which you simply did not do. She looked at Jamie. 'Can you tell?'

Jamie reached for the water jug. 'Yes. I knew somebody at music college who felt perpetually guilty about the smallest things. He had been to one of those Catholic boarding schools and had been made to think about the implications for his soul of the very smallest things. His thoughts, for example. He felt guilty about his thoughts. All the time.'

Isabel knew what Jamie meant. So am I neurotic? she wondered. She thought uncharitable thoughts – about Dove, for example. Should she feel guilty about that? At the height of his plot against her, she had imagined Dove being exposed as a plagiarist. Then she had imagined herself writing a critical review of one of his books and demolishing it, chapter by chapter, elegantly, like a matador with a pen. Surely we should not worry too much about our uncharitable thoughts, as long as we did not act on them. And yet that was not the understanding that people had had in the past: did not the Book of Common Prayer say, 'I have sinned in thought, word and deed'? Or had we released ourselves from the tyranny of worrying about the things that the mind came up with? Isabel felt uncertain; the niggling doubt remained that perhaps there was something in purity of mind after all.

Edward Mendelson had an early plane to catch, back to London and then to New York, and so he did not stay for coffee after dinner. Isabel said goodbye to him at the front door, while Jamie remained in the kitchen to clear up. Edward said to her, 'I'm so pleased to see you happy. I can tell that, you know – you're very happy.'

Isabel smiled. 'There's every reason for me to be happy,' she said. 'I have a job I love, a nice man, a son. This house.' She paused. 'Not that one should enumerate one's good fortune in this life. Nemesis listens for that sort of thing, I fear.'

'She has far greater fish to fry,' said Edward. 'Terrible politicians. Dictators. Actors who have grown too big for their boots. Your claims are pretty modest by comparison. Hardly a trace of hubris, I would have thought.'

He walked down the path. It was barely dark, as it was midsummer now, and even at ten in the evening the sky was suffused with an attenuated glow. The air was warm, almost balmy, and the leaves of the trees and shrubs, the rhododendrons, the azaleas, were heavy and static, as if weighed down by the air. I am very fortunate, thought Isabel, as she made her way back to the kitchen where Jamie, who had stacked the dishes in the dishwasher, was standing in the middle of the room, stretching his arms up above him in an exaggerated yawn. The act made his shirt come up over his midriff, which was flat and muscled. *To me the entirely beautiful*, thought Isabel. He watched her, and let his arms fall. He has guessed what was in my mind, she thought.

'I just saw Brother Fox outside the window,' he said.

'Trotting along the top of the neighbours' garden wall, bold as brass.'

'Did he see you?'

'No. I don't think so. He had places to go.'

'*For he had many a mile to go that night*,' said Isabel, looking out of the window, '*Before he reached the town-o.*'

'I must learn the words of that song,' said Jamie. 'We can sing it to Charlie.'

She waited for him to say something more, about a fox, or a painting of a fox, but he did not. He went over to her though, and put his arms around her, and she closed her eyes and felt him against her, this young man whom she could not quite believe she possessed, whose every act, whose every word, no matter how banal, no matter how inconsequential, was precious to her. That was love, she supposed, elevating the ordinary into something beyond itself, and carrying one along with the entire absurd enterprise.

14

Eddie had predicted that Saturday would be busy, and it was. Isabel liked Saturdays, but not quite so much, she thought, if she had to work. And yet even a working Saturday seemed subtly different from a weekday; the people who came into the delicatessen drifted in, rather than entered with purpose, and although she and Eddie were busy, there was a last-day-of-term feel about their work. At five o'clock they would shut the door for the weekend – or what remained of it – and that knowledge made the work easier.

Eddie did not say much to Isabel, but seemed to be in a good mood and had apparently forgotten their discussion of the five hundred pounds. Isabel had not – obviously not – and was still thinking of the lie he had told her: that ridiculous story of his father's hip operation and wanting the money for that. On subsequent reflection she had worked out where the money had gone, and it made her angry just to think about it. Eddie had a new girlfriend, who had come round to see him in the delicatessen on more than one occasion, including one afternoon that week. He had seemed embarrassed by her visit and had shooed her out after a few minutes, but Isabel could tell that he was proud of her; perhaps proud of the mere fact that he had a girlfriend at all.

But Isabel had thought: drugs, and the more she pondered it, the more she thought, drugs. The girl was thin, dressed entirely in black, and had a prominent piercing on her lower lip. All of that could be a matter of fashion, of course – the Goth style – but there had been her expression, which Isabel found unsettling. It was that anxiety, that itchiness, that goes with the chemical personality. And she sniffed too.

So Eddie had given the five hundred pounds into the hands of this young woman. *My* five hundred pounds, thought Isabel. She looked at Eddie, who was cutting cheese for a customer. There was no evidence that he was on anything, except cheese, perhaps; she had noticed how he always scooped up the fragments from the cutting board and popped them into his mouth. He was on cheese and the girl was on something stronger.

Isabel decided that she would tackle him about the money and ask for it back. But then she decided she would not. She simply did not have the heart – or was it the stomach? – to engage with Eddie over this. If he had given the money to the girl, then he would never be able to get it back; and if he could not get it back, then any demand from her would put him under considerable pressure, and he was too insecure for that. Besides, she had given him the money, she had not lent it to him; she had given it, and one could not ask for gifts to be returned unless there had been a very explicit condition attached to the donation. And she had not said anything about that, as far as she recalled: she had pressed the money on him; she had urged him to take it.

While Isabel spent her Saturday working in the delicatessen,

Jamie looked after Charlie. It was another warm day in a run of fine days, and he took Charlie for a long walk in his back sling round the Braid Hills, on the southern edge of the city. Up there, at the top of Buckstone Snab, the air was cooler, with a breeze blowing down from Stirlingshire and the hills of Perthshire beyond. Charlie started to shiver, and his small, snub nose looked red. They returned, back to Isabel's green Swedish car – which Jamie now drove too – parked in the car park of the golf club below.

When they got back to the house, Jamie noticed a car parked slightly further up the street, in which a man was sitting. While he was getting Charlie out of the car, the door of the other vehicle opened and the man got out and approached Jamie in the drive. He was a tall man, somewhere in his early forties, dressed in the style that Isabel described as casual-smart-verging-on-the-formal, which meant a tie and a jacket, not a suit, but almost, since the trousers and the jacket were close together in shade. He spoke in the accent of Aberdeen, which Jamie associated with a certain caution and canniness. Aberdeen people had the reputation of not wasting their words, nor anything really; it was a cold part of the country, a place of fishermen and offshore oil people, used to sea and biting winds and hardship.

'I'm looking for Miss Dalhousie,' he said. 'I rang the bell, but thought that she might be out shopping. I've been waiting.'

Jamie wiped at Charlie's now-streaming nose. 'I'm afraid that you've missed her. She's working today. She helps somebody out in a delicatessen.'

'I'd like to see her,' said the man, reaching into his pocket for a card. He proffered the card to Jamie, who took it and read it.

'David McLean. You're a lawyer.'

'Yes. I was hoping to have a word with Miss Dalhousie today, if at all possible. I have to go down to London next week for several days, and I thought I might just be able to catch her on a Saturday.'

Jamie shrugged. He knew that Isabel had dealings with various lawyers over financial matters, and he assumed that David McLean was one of these. 'Saturday's their busy day, but you can go along and see if she has a moment.'

Jamie explained where the delicatessen was, and David McLean nodded. 'I know the place. We use it from time to time. We don't live far away.' He paused. 'Thank you. Nice wee boy. He is a boy, isn't he?'

'He is.'

'What's his name?'

'Charlie.'

'Hallo, Charlie.'

Charlie looked at the lawyer with that intense scrutinising stare of the very young. David McLean looked away, as if he were embarrassed by something; Jamie noticed this. Then he thanked Jamie and walked off, back to his car. Jamie hugged Charlie to him; the smooth cheek felt cold against his skin, and he reached for the little hand in its mitten. Even in summer, a small child was such a scrap of humanity that he might easily be chilled by a breeze. And Scottish weather was so unpredictable; a warm, clear day could become almost Arctic if a wind blew up from the wrong direction. He needed to get Charlie inside and put him down for a sleep, in his warm room where the afternoon sun came in the window. For a moment he wondered whether he should telephone Isabel in advance of David McLean's reaching her, but then he put the thought out of his mind. Charlie had started to complain; a cold wind was one thing, waiting for his lunch quite another.

'No,' said Eddie. 'You can't return cheese.'

The customer, a young woman wearing a knitted hat, held out the offending parcel. 'But smell it. Go on, smell it.'

Eddie took the cheese and sniffed it, watched by another, slightly amused customer. The woman in the knitted hat watched him, waiting for confirmation of her complaint.

Eddie lowered the parcel. 'But that's how this cheese always smells. It's called Pont l'Evêque. It's French. French cheese smells. They like it that way.'

The woman snatched the parcel back from him and sniffed at it herself. 'You're telling me that this is how it's meant to be? I bet that if I took a culture from it, it would show all sorts of things. There are European Union regulations about that sort of thing, you know. This cheese should be called salmonella.'

'It's not called salmonella,' said Eddie. 'It's—'

'I know it's not called that,' interjected the woman. 'I said that's what it *should* be called. Like gorgonzola.'

Isabel had come up behind Eddie. She glanced at the cheese and whispered to him, 'Take it back.'

Eddie cocked his head to listen to her, but then turned back to face the customer. 'If you don't like smelly cheese you should get something different. Cheddar, maybe.'

Isabel intervened. 'I think we can do a refund,' she said. 'Or we can give you another cheese. Have you tried this one? This is an Italian cheese, Grana, which is just like Parmesan, but much cheaper. Here, try a little bit.'

She cut a small piece of cheese from a block on the counter

and handed it, on the knife, to the young woman. Eddie glowered, but the young woman, mollified, nodded enthusiastically. 'I really like that,' she said. 'And it doesn't stink.' She threw a glance at Eddie as she made the last remark, and he blushed.

Eddie watched as Isabel cut the Grana for the young woman. From a corner of the shop, David McLean also watched, and when Isabel had finished attending to the customer he came forward to the counter.

'Isabel Dalhousie?'

Isabel was surprised to be addressed by name in the delicatessen, where she thought few people, other than the most regular of customers, knew who she was. 'Yes.' It was guarded, as if she might assent now to be Isabel Dalhousie, but reserved the right to be somebody else if necessary.

David McLean fished his card from his pocket and passed it over to her. 'I wonder if we could possibly have a quick word,' he said, nodding in the direction of the coffee tables, none of which was occupied.

Isabel looked at the card. 'We're very busy,' she said. 'And there are just two of us at the moment.'

Eddie, standing just behind her, interrupted. 'That's all right. I'll cope.' He spoke with a sense of injured innocence; Isabel might refund cheese unnecessarily, against his better judgement, but *he* was not one to bear a grudge or be petty.

She looked at Eddie. 'Are you sure?'

'Yes.'

Isabel turned back to face David McLean. 'As it happens, I'm ready for a coffee. Would you like one?'

'I'll make them,' offered Eddie.

Isabel did not argue, but loosened her apron and went over to sit with David McLean at the table near the window. The lawyer waited courteously while she took a seat before lowering himself into a chair. She noted that, and the shoes he was wearing – expensive black brogues, highly polished.

'Your friend told me that you would be here,' he said. 'I hope you don't mind my coming to see you at work.'

'My friend?'

'At the house. Jamie. Your young musician.'

'I see.'

McLean was resting his left hand on the top of the table. Isabel noticed that there was a ring on the little finger, a signet ring, on which there was engraved in the gold a tiny axe. Isabel knew that this was the symbol of the clan McLean; Charlie McLean had told her that when she had seen the axe on his kilt pin. David McLean took his hand off the table.

'I'll come right to the point,' he said. 'My firm acts for a pharmaceutical firm. They are not based here in Scotland – they are based abroad, in fact. But we represent their London lawyers in Scotland.'

Isabel hardly had to ask, but did nevertheless; more to say something than to find out the answer. 'The people who make the antibiotic that . . .'

'Yes,' said David McLean. 'Precisely.'

He put his hand back on the table. The ring caught a shaft of sun coming through the window, and glinted briefly.

'As you know,' he went on, 'there was a very unfortunate incident not all that long ago. The doctor in question was represented by somebody else in the proceedings before the medical authorities; we merely watched the situation for our own clients. Obviously they were very concerned about the reputation of their product.'

'Obviously.'

'Yes. People are very quick to blame manufacturers for things that go wrong. And this seems to apply particularly to those who manufacture drugs. That's curious, isn't it? Everybody wants new drugs to be made available, but nobody seems to want to accept the risk that goes with putting these things on the market. And it's always the fault of the drug companies, isn't it, when something goes wrong? Or that's what the press implies.'

Isabel had forgotten about the coffee, but now it arrived. Eddie put two mugs on the table, glancing with distaste at the lawyer as he did so.

McLean lifted the mug to his lips and sipped at the hot, milky liquid, looking at Isabel as he did so. It seemed to her that he was waiting for her to agree with him, with what he had just said.

She blew across the surface of her coffee to cool it. 'Perhaps we shouldn't be so surprised,' she said. 'The pharmaceutical companies make very considerable profits. They are quite simply rich. People have never liked—'

He interrupted her, smiling as he spoke. 'People have never liked the rich? I suppose you should understand that, Miss Dalhousie.'

She caught her breath, and she thought of saying to him, 'That remark is unprofessional.' But she did not. He had unwittingly – perhaps – declared his hostility, but she did not want to engage. She looked over towards the counter, where Eddie was standing, dealing with a customer. Suddenly, she felt vulnerable. This stranger knew who she was; he had been to the house; he knew her personal circumstances. Or did he? Had he merely seen the house and concluded that anybody who lived in a large self-contained Victorian house in that street, in that part of town, must have money in the bank? It did not require any great skill to reach that conclusion.

'The point is that public understanding of the industry is less than impressive,' David McLean went on. 'I take it that you know that the return on capital for the pharmaceutical industry in this country is about seventeen per cent, which is very much in line with other large industries. And I take it that you know that one third of profits are put back into research and development – so that there can be new drugs at the end of the day.' He paused, watching her. 'But that's not the point of my visit. The point is that there's a lot of pointing of fingers and not a great deal of solid information out there. Obviously my clients have to watch situations where their position is potentially under scrutiny.'

Isabel glanced at her watch – pointedly.

'All right,' he said. 'I don't want to keep you. This is my concern: you have been involving yourself, I understand, in this very unfortunate business of Dr Marcus Moncrieff.'

Isabel said nothing. She was thinking about what interest the company who made the drug in question would have in whether or not Marcus had been negligent in failing to check the results from the laboratory. They would have benefited from this negligence, as it meant that the drug was considered safe and could have continued to be used. Their problems only started when it was discovered that a much smaller dose had caused the side effects.

David McLean leaned forward slightly. He lowered his voice. 'We – or shall I say, our clients – would prefer it if you did not disturb the result of the internal enquiry. In other words, we don't think that it's helpful for you to do anything that might reopen this case. That would not be in Marcus Moncrieff's interests, I think.'

She stared at him; to give them the benefit of the doubt, perhaps it would not have occurred to them that somebody might have interfered with the figures. She went over in her mind what might have happened. The patients may have taken a normal overdose. Norrie might then have changed the figures so that it looked as if they had had a massive overdose. He might have guessed, correctly, that Marcus would dismiss the risk, and then, once he had made his report, he could be exposed as being negligent. But even if Norrie had done this, it would have had nothing to do with the pharmaceutical company; they had done nothing wrong. Unless, of course . . . It dawned on her suddenly. Norrie might have had a very different motive for falsifying the results from the one she had been thinking about. He might have done it not in order to discredit his uncle, but because somebody had made it worth his while to do so. And the obvious people to have done that would be the drug's makers. It would suit them perfectly to have the side effects cases shown to have been the result of a grossly excessive overdose rather than a more likely one. Of course it would, she thought, of course it would.

She took a deep breath to calm herself. 'Doesn't it offend you,' she asked, 'that an innocent man should have his career brought to an end over something he did not do? You're a lawyer, aren't you? Doesn't that offend everything your profession stands for?'

David McLean seemed slightly taken aback by her question, and for a few moments he did not reply. Then, 'Of course it would offend me. But we're not talking about an innocent man here. We're talking about a man who was grossly negligent, a man who should have known much better.'

'Unless he wasn't careless at all,' said Isabel quickly. 'Unless somebody else changed the figures, later on, in order to make it look as if he had been careless.'

David McLean was quite still. 'What do you mean by that?'

Isabel felt her courage come flooding back. 'I mean exactly what I said. What if somebody else, encouraged, shall we say, by another, falsified the figures to make it look as if the drug had been administered in far greater quantities than it actually had been? Do you see what I mean?'

This last question came out as a challenge, although she had not intended it to sound that way. I have virtually accused his clients, she thought. I could hardly make it more obvious.

David McLean must have reached the same conclusion. He glanced out of the window, briefly, then let his gaze return to Isabel. She felt uneasy, but she was angry now and would not be intimidated.

'I shall do exactly as I please, Mr McLean,' she said, rising to her feet to indicate that their conversation was over.

He was thrown off balance. 'Be careful,' he said quietly. 'Just be careful.'

Isabel, who had started to walk back to the counter, spun round to face him. 'Are you threatening me?'

He looked anxiously in the direction of a customer who was examining a packet of dried pasta which he had taken off a shelf. The customer looked up, surprised, and then quickly went back to studying the packet. Edinburgh was not a place where one showed a reaction to that which one overheard. 'Of course not,' David McLean said. 'Don't be ridiculous. I'm just telling you to be careful.'

Eddie was watching her from the counter. He had just fin-ished serving a customer, and when she joined him he was

185

wiping his hands on a piece of paper towel. 'Are you all right?' he whispered.

She felt a sudden fondness for Eddie, in spite of the five hundred pounds. He was concerned for her, and she found his anxiety touching: this mixed-up, damaged boy was actually concerned for her. She reached out and touched Eddie on the forearm. 'I'm fine, Eddie. I'm fine.'

Eddie glowered at David McLean, who was now leaving the shop. 'What did he want?'

'He wanted me to . . .' Isabel trailed off. It was too complicated, and she was wrestling with a question. He seemed to know about Jamie; he knew his name and that he was a musician. She wondered whether Jamie had told him this, or whether he had found it out. And if he had found it out, then he must have gone to some lengths to do so, which meant that he was taking a close interest in her affairs. He had said that he was not threatening her, but why else, she wondered, would he tell her to be careful? A warning? You simply did not walk up to somebody you had never met, reveal that you knew all about her, and then say, Watch out. That happened in novels, perhaps, but not in real life. And I am real, thought Isabel, and this life, this delicatessen, this problematic young man beside me, are all real and immediate – part of the brief, sparkling privilege that I have of consciousness in a universe where, as far as we could tell, there were few signs of consciousness. Looked at in this way, a few words of threat from a man in highly polished brogues and wearing a Scottish clan ring were nothing.

She turned to Eddie. 'We don't have to worry about him,' she said. 'But thank you, anyway. We're on the same side, aren't we, Eddie? You and me.'

And then she leaned forward and planted a kiss on his cheek.

He gave a start, as if he had suddenly had a jolt of electricity, and Isabel wondered: did that girl with the piercings not kiss him?

Eddie looked at her. 'I wanted to say sorry properly,' he muttered. 'So . . . I'm sorry. I'm useless at telling people things.'

She put an arm around his shoulder. She wanted to. 'You're not useless.'

Eddie fumbled in his pocket. 'And here's the money I owe you. I gave it to my dad for his hip operation.' He lowered his eyes. He was ashamed. 'And he spent some of it. That's why it's taken time to pay you back.'

Isabel was appalled, and in her abhorrence could say nothing. Two wrongs had been done to this wronged young man: she had written him off as a liar and his father had misused the money he had given him – gambling, drink, it did not really matter how. She stared at him.

'Anyway,' Eddie said to her, 'he's been given a date for his hip now. It's in two months. So he's in a better temper.'

'Pain is an odd thing,' said Isabel. 'It makes people do things they wouldn't otherwise do. You know that, don't you?'

Eddie nodded. He knew.

15

She was in the garden the next morning, Sunday, with Charlie when she made her decision about Christopher Dove's paper on the Trolley Problem. It was nothing that Charlie had said – he had several sounds at his command, one of which could have been 'Dove', but was more likely the precursor of 'Daddy'; certainly a d came into it. And there was another sound, n-ish in tone, which could have been an incipient no; a useful word for a baby resisting the plans that the world, in the shape of mother, had for him. There was definitely an n sound, and had the d sound been combined with it, then there would have been no doubt that Charlie had said: Dove? No! But he had been silent, sitting on a blanket spread out on the lawn, wearing a small, rather ridiculous hat and his McPherson tartan rompers, gazing thoughtfully at a nearby lavender bush about which a couple of bees were circling. He has seen the bees, thought Isabel, and one day – not just yet – he will have to learn the lesson that we all learn about bees. And hot things; and loss, perhaps; and the fact that not all stories have happy endings. But there was time enough for that; for the moment these bees were entirely innocent sources of noise for him, enough to keep him busy while Isabel, from her corner of the blanket, contemplated her response to Dove.

The previous day she had received the second report on Dove's article from a professor of philosophy in Glasgow. 'Not the best paper I have ever read,' wrote the professor. 'The author tries his best to extract further mileage from a trolley ride that is, in my view, already far too complicated. How that trolley, burdened as it is with such a weight of philosophical commentary, even manages to leave its depot, defeats me. Its journey should be terminated.' The verdict was put politely, but it was clearly a negative one. Two-nil against Dove, thought Isabel.

She would have to reject Dove's paper. She had reached this position by asking herself what she would have done had the paper been from somebody whom she did not know. Her procedure in such a case would be to follow the recommendations of the reviewers, and she had now had two votes for rejection. If she ignored these – with a view to avoiding recriminations from Dove – then by that very act she would be doing an injustice to all those others whom she had rejected on the basis of bad reports. Every one of them would have dealt with her on an implicit understanding that there were procedures for the acceptance of papers that were consistently applied. She would be breaking faith with them if she did anything but that; it was simply not an option.

Now she mentally composed the letter she would write. The first hurdle was the second word. Dear Christopher was one option; Dear Professor Dove was another; the difference between the two was obvious, and represented the difference between friendship and acquaintance. Another option altogether was Dear

Dove; an old-fashioned mode of address that had virtually died out but which was still used here and there by older scholars. In Isabel's mouth the surname on its own would sound strange, and she could not bring herself to call him Christopher. So it was Dear Professor Dove, and with that resolved, the rest proved easy:

It was most thoughtful of you to offer me this excellent piece on the Trolley Problem. How these old problems still provide us with fresh food for thought! That is what I thought, at least, but then *quot homines tot sententiae*! (as I'm sure you will agree), and my view was not shared, alas, by the reviewers (two of them) who felt that your piece was not sufficiently original or insightful to merit publication. I was astonished, but I felt that I really had to abide by their decision, as not to do so would be unfair to those other authors (of similarly eminently publishable pieces) who have been turned down on the grounds of referees' reports. Of course, these things are subjective, as is shown by the fact that you have had other offers to publish this piece. I believe that you should take those, and that is why I am writing to you so soon after receiving the unfavourable reports. I would not wish to hold you back from anxious publishers elsewhere. I shall certainly look out for the article's appearance in the United States – you forgot to tell me, by the way, exactly who has offered for it; I assume that it's the *American Philosophical Quarterly* or *Ethics* – somebody of that order. But wherever it ends up, I am sure that it will attract the attention it deserves.

Yours sincerely,

Isabel Dalhousie

The plotting of the letter was a delicious pleasure, particularly the phrase *it will attract the attention it deserves*. That meant everything, or nothing, the implication in this case, if Dove was capable of reading between the lines, being nothing. She looked at Charlie, who was still staring at the bees, and then reprimanded herself; the contemplation of Dove's discomfiture gave pleasure, but it was not a pleasure that she could allow herself. We have a moral duty to forgive; she knew that. To forgive Christopher Dove, who had attempted to engineer a coup against her at the *Review*, to throw her out of her editorial chair? Who blatantly lied to her about his article being accepted for publication elsewhere? Yes. Even Dove.

So she decided the letter would be brief and to the point.

Dear Christopher Dove (a compromise),

   I'm so sorry that we shall not be able to publish your paper. I have taken two referees' opinions – in accordance with normal practice – and I'm afraid that both were against publication. I'm sure that the paper has many merits and will find a home elsewhere.

   Yours sincerely,
   Isabel Dalhousie

'Letters with moral merit,' she said to Charlie, 'are often very dull. Humour, Charlie, usually needs a victim.'

Charlie, hearing this gurgling sound from his mother, turned and looked at her briefly before returning to his scrutiny of the bees.

'You're very wise, Charlie,' Isabel continued. 'Bees are such interesting creatures, with all their intense activity. They have so few doubts. Look at them. They are so thoroughly accepting of their place in the bee order. Workers. Queen. It's interesting, Charlie, that the queen is the boss. Always a female bee. A model for matriarchies everywhere.'

'Exactly,' a voice said. 'Exactly.'

Isabel looked up. Cat was standing immediately behind her. 'You're back!'

Cat looked down on them. 'Does Charlie agree with you all the time?'

Isabel laughed. 'You are meant to talk to them, you know,' she said. 'Even if they don't understand.'

And if you did not? she wondered. She had heard a depressing talk on the radio which revealed that many children these days learned language not from their parents, who barely spoke to them, but from the television. So a child's first words might be, 'Here is the news . . .'

Cat walked across the blanket, bent down, and tickled Charlie under the chin. But she did not kiss him. 'Yes, you should talk to them. But surely you should say something they understand.'

'Remember James the Fourth,' said Isabel. 'He thought that if children heard nothing at all, no language, then they would naturally speak Hebrew. He thought it the natural language.'

Cat made a non-committal sound – possibly Hebrew.

'And, as you know,' Isabel went on, 'he put a baby out on one of those islands in the Forth – just out there – with a dumb woman to look after him. The king of Scotland's big experiment – to see if the boy would speak Hebrew.'

'How cruel,' said Cat. She did not sound interested.

Isabel shot a glance at her niece. It seemed inconceivable to her, not to be intrigued by the world. But Cat really was not. She related only to those things that impinged upon her immediate life, Isabel thought. The delicatessen. Men. What else? 'I suppose I was really talking to myself,' said Isabel. 'You know how people do that. They talk at great length to their cat or dog, but it's merely a way of talking to themselves.'

It was as if Cat had not heard what Isabel said. She sat down on the blanket and turned to look at Charlie. 'Bees, Charlie. Those are bees. Bees.'

'I already told him that,' said Isabel. 'Charlie does not need people to repeat things to him.' She looked appraisingly at Cat, who had caught the sun in Sri Lanka – not badly, but it had been there, across her face.

'The sun signs his presence,' muttered Isabel.

'What?'

'You've caught the sun. Just a bit. It's nice to see you, anyway. I didn't expect to see you so soon. You must be tired.'

Cat raised an arm to brush the hair off her brow. She is very beautiful, thought Isabel. That's why all these men fall for her. It's something to do with her profile, her nose. How strange that a nose can be the determinant of happiness or unhappiness; a few centimetres more gristle in the wrong place, just that, and Cat might have battled to find one man, let alone . . . how many boyfriends had there been over the last five years? Five?

'I slept on the plane,' said Cat. 'Somehow. The woman sitting next to me was tiny, and the aisle was on the other side, and so I was able to sleep.' She closed her eyes and turned her brow to the sun. Isabel watched her.

Charlie had stopped looking at the bees and was now crawling towards Cat. He was distracted, though, by a small stuffed dog which was lying on the blanket. He reached for it and began to suck one of its legs.

'Thank you for your message,' said Isabel. 'You obviously enjoyed Sri Lanka.'

'Loved it,' said Cat. 'I want to go back. The people. The place. Everything. I want to go back to Galle. It's a place down in the south. An old fort.'

Isabel visualised a map of Sri Lanka. It was tear-shaped, was it not? The tear off the coast of India. 'Well,' she said. 'That's next year's trip sorted out for you.'

Cat opened her eyes. 'Not next year. Sooner. Really soon.'

For a moment Isabel was silent as she contemplated the implications of this. Who would be in charge of the delicatessen while Cat was away? Then she asked, 'Really soon means when? Next month?'

'Maybe,' said Cat. 'But don't worry. I won't expect you to look after the shop. I'm going to advertise for somebody. A manager.'

Isabel looked surprised. From time to time Cat had extra people working in the delicatessen – there had been that Australian girl who had been so friendly with Eddie – but she had always maintained that another full-time salary would push the business into loss.

'I thought that margins were too tight,' said Isabel. 'A manager?'

Cat did not look at her when she replied. 'Change of plans. I think that I might be spending more time in Sri Lanka. I'll need somebody who can run the shop full-time. Somebody who can supervise Eddie.' She let this sink in before continuing: 'Actually, I've met somebody there. He's an artist. He's done up one of those houses in the Old Fort. It was a Dutch merchant's house – a lovely place.'

Isabel listened attentively. 'I've seen pictures of the town. I looked it up after you went. It looks—'

Cat did not give her time to finish. 'He's an Australian. From Melbourne. He's lived in Sri Lanka for six years now. Quite a few foreigners live in Galle, you know. It's the . . . the most gorgeous place. Courtyards. Frangipani trees. It's so beautiful.'

Isabel kept her voice even. She had her differences with Cat, but she did not want to lose her. 'You make me want to go there.'

'You'd love it,' said Cat.

'I'm sure I would.' Isabel let a few moments pass. 'When will you go?'

Cat shrugged. 'In six weeks. Maybe two months. It depends on who I find for the job and when that person can start.'

'And will you . . .?' The question was left unfinished, but its meaning was clear.

'For ever? No, I don't think so. Simon likes it there, but he likes to travel. He thought that he might spend some time here in Edinburgh. He's never been to Scotland, but his father was Scottish, and he said that he always wanted to see it.'

Charlie had now abandoned the stuffed dog and started to crawl back towards Isabel. She reached out and put him on her knee. Cat watched idly; she was still in Sri Lanka.

Suddenly Isabel said something that she had not intended to say. She did that from time to time, as we all do, the words coming out unbidden. 'Wouldn't you like to settle down, Cat? Wouldn't you like a baby? Just like Charlie?'

Cat froze. Isabel, realising what she had said, busied herself with Charlie, adjusting his hat, which had fallen down over his eyes. 'Sorry,' she said. 'I didn't mean to say that.'

'Then what did you mean?'

'Oh, I suppose I've been worried about you. I want you to

be happy, obviously I do. And, well, look at me. I've got Charlie now . . .' She was making it worse.

'I can settle down when I want,' said Cat. 'Any time.'

Isabel was placatory. 'Of course you could.'

'And you don't need to have a baby to settle down. Some men may not want one, you know. We don't have to tie them down with babies.'

Isabel said nothing. Cat's meaning was clear. She – Isabel – was being accused of tying Jamie down; exactly the thing that she had tried not to do. 'Is that how it looks to you?' she asked quietly. 'Do you think that I've tied Jamie down?'

Cat hesitated. 'Maybe. Maybe, a bit. After all, he's much younger, isn't he?'

'Do you think I'm not aware of that?'

Cat rose to her feet. 'Look, I'm tired. And I don't think this is getting us anywhere. I came to thank you for looking after the shop. I'm really grateful. And I've brought you something from Sri Lanka.' She fished into a bag that she had brought with her and extricated a box of tea. 'White tea,' she said. 'It's a great delicacy. It comes from the smallest leaves of the tea plant, when they're still buds.'

Isabel took the box of tea and thanked her. Then Cat left, and Isabel sat on the rug with Charlie. She embraced him, gently, feeling his breath against her cheek. She had tied nobody down. Not Jamie. Not Grace. And she would not tie her son down either. They were all free and would always be. That's what I believe in, she told herself. That, and you, Charlie, you, my darling.

She went inside. It was Charlie's lunchtime, and she prepared some minced lamb and vegetable puree for him, which he

196

gobbled down with enthusiasm. Then it was time for his afternoon sleep; he rubbed his eyes in his struggle to remain awake.
'No need to stay awake, my darling,' she said. 'Land of Nod for
you.'

'Nn,' said Charlie.

'Nn? Of course, you're right. Nn.'

He dropped off almost immediately, and Isabel made her way
downstairs to her study. Jamie was in Glasgow for the day, playing with Scottish Opera in a walk-through of a new
production. He would be back in time for dinner, he had said,
and they would go out together; Grace had offered to babysit.

She sat at her desk and had begun to write her letter to
Dove – the restrained letter – when she saw that the small
red light of her answering machine was blinking. She had
cleared it of messages earlier that day; something must have
come in while she was sitting out in the garden. She wondered
whether it was Jamie; occasionally he got away in good time
and caught an earlier train. Or Grace, to say that she could
not babysit? She had an aunt in Leith who was unwell at the
moment and she had warned Isabel that she might have to
spend the evening with her rather than babysitting Charlie.

Isabel pressed the play button.

'Hi. I hope I have the right number. I've tried the other one
you gave me and there was no reply. I hope you get this. Good
news. That audition in Boston – I spoke to Tom, the guy I
talked about, and he said that they'll hear you. He says they're
in funds right now and they'll pay your fare – economy, sorry –
week after next, as planned. I'll come too. Hold your hand, so
to speak. But they need to know real soon. So call me when
you get back and then I'll call Tom. Okay?'

Isabel's finger stayed where it was, resting against the play

197

button. Nick Smart. How easy to get numbers mixed up, even, it would seem, when you are a very self-possessed composer whose life, it appears to others, moves on well-oiled tracks.

Jamie had said nothing to her about this. Nothing. And where was that picture of Brother Fox? Had she made a dreadful mistake? And did he really love her, or was she just labouring under some huge delusion?

She looked at the beginnings of the letter to Dove on her computer screen, as if that might distract her from the cold dread that had suddenly come upon her. She moved her hands back to the keyboard. Why did people hurt one another? Why did we punish one another in all the inventive ways we had devised for the purpose? She stared at the screen through her tears and decided she would not bring disappointment; she would not be the agent of Nemesis, not this time, not now. 'Dear Christopher,' she wrote. 'Thank you for sending me that piece on the Trolley Problem. Yes, we shall publish this. Not this issue but the next. Warmest wishes, Isabel.'

She pressed the key that would print the letter on the headed note-paper of the *Review*. Then she stood up, but sat down again almost immediately. She did not know what to do. She felt as if she wanted to run out of the house, to get away from everything; but Charlie was upstairs, and she could not. She was tied down. Jamie was free, as she wanted him to be, but she was tied down.

16

Jamie was on the train that left Glasgow at six o'clock. He arrived back at the house shortly after seven, letting himself in by the front door and going straight upstairs to see if Charlie was still awake. The nursery was in semi-darkness, the shutters closed, the only light being that from the dim bulb that calmed Charlie through the watches of the night. He could tell from his breathing that Charlie was deeply asleep, and when he looked down he saw the small head on the mattress, his eyes closed, his mouth open in repose. He bent down and planted the lightest of kisses on his son's forehead, or just above it, as he did not want to wake him. There was the smell of soap, of down, of washed wool blanket, of a tiny life.

He found Isabel in the kitchen, leaning against the polished steel guardrail of the cooking range, paging through a magazine. She looked up when he came in, and he sensed immediately that something was wrong. At least Charlie was all right; it had nothing to do with that. The *Review*? She had been worrying over some business with Dove. Or that doctor and his troubles; Isabel could get caught up in the problems of others to the point where she allowed them to destroy her peace of mind. Maybe it was that.

'Is something wrong?'

She shook her head, far too quickly, he thought.

He crossed the room. 'Yes, there is. Of course there is.'

She avoided meeting his gaze, and that, he thought, was another sign. He was standing in front of her now and took the magazine from her hands; he saw that it was upside down.

'What is it, Isabel? Please tell me.'

She looked down at the floor steadfastly. 'There was a message for you on the answering machine.'

He frowned. 'What about?'

'About Boston,' she said. 'About . . .'

He took her hand. 'Oh,' he said.

She waited for him to continue, but he was silent.

'Nick Smart,' she said. 'He telephoned to say that the audition was on.'

Jamie looked at her uncomprehendingly. 'What audition?'

'The audition he's arranged for you.' She paused and their eyes met, but only briefly. 'So if they like you, presumably you'll go and work there. Live there.'

Slowly the look on Jamie's face changed from incomprehension to understanding. 'That audition's not for me,' he said quietly. 'And the message wasn't for me either. I think he dialled the wrong number.'

'Yes he did,' said Isabel. 'He thought this was your flat.'

Jamie took her hand. She tried to take it away from him, but he held on, tightly. 'No, don't. Don't. Just listen to me, Isabel. That audition is for Will. You know, the oboist. The one you heard play that solo at the Queen's Hall last time. He and Nick have been hitting it off rather well recently, and Will said that

Nick was arranging for him to have an audition over in Boston. I only half-listened at the time, but it was something to that effect.' He stopped. He was trying to work out why Nick had telephoned the house. 'And so I think what happened is that he meant to phone Will but phoned us instead. He's got this number. I gave him both. He must have looked the wrong one up.'

He felt Isabel stop trying to release her hand. She did not care how the error had come about; the important thing was that it was an error. 'So you're not going to Boston?' she said.

'Of course not. And I certainly wouldn't go anywhere at Nick's suggestion.' He paused. 'There's something about him that makes me uncomfortable, you know. He's sarcastic about other people. Belittles them. But I don't want to be rude to him.'

Isabel gave him her other hand. He was cold from the walk up from Haymarket, and she squeezed his hands to warm them up.

'You're kind,' she said. 'You're kind to him. To me. To everyone.'

'I'm not . . .' He was embarrassed, and turned away. It was now sinking in that she had believed him to be about to desert her. How could she think that?

Isabel put her arms around him. 'Please,' she said. 'Please forgive me . . . forgive me for even thinking that you could hide something from me. I'm so sorry.'

'I wouldn't . . . I really wouldn't even think . . .'

'Of course you wouldn't. It's all in my mind. I'm the stupid one.'

They stood in silence, and then, after a few minutes, he reminded her that they were due to go out to dinner; that he needed to take a shower and that she would want to get dressed. 'Also,' he said. 'Also, I've got a little present for you.'

Her heart gave a leap; the picture of Brother Fox, and she had almost spoiled the occasion of its presentation by accusing him of being about to desert her . . . and Charlie.

He left the room and came back with something in his hands. A small bunch of flowers, freesias, carefully done up in the florist's thin printed foil, their strong, sweet scent rising from the packaging; a simple bunch of flowers.

She kissed him on the cheek. 'A real surprise,' she said, adding, 'in more ways than one.'

'Why?'

She hesitated. Why had she added anything? Thank you would have been enough. 'I was expecting something else, I suppose. These are very nice, but I was expecting something else.'

It was too late to withdraw the remark, and she found that she did not have the heart to lie. So when he asked her what she had been expecting, she told him what she had thought that it might be.

'I thought you were going to give me a picture,' she said, and, seeing his surprise, added, 'a picture of a fox.'

'A fox?'

'Yes. I'm sorry. I saw it more or less by mistake.'

'I thought that you would like these flowers,' said Jamie.

'Of course I do,' she said. 'And I should never have said that I was expecting something else.'

Jamie began to smile. 'On the other hand . . . Or, shall I say, *in* the other hand . . .' He had been holding the painting in his other hand, concealed behind his back, and now he gave it to her, a small parcel wrapped in green paper, about which a silver ribbon had been inexpertly tied. Men are not good at tying ribbons, thought Isabel; but she would not have it otherwise – she would not change this inadequately tied ribbon for anything else.

'I knew that you knew about it,' Jamie said. 'Robin showed it to you, as I'd asked him to. I had forgotten to tell you about it, and so I decided to add an element of anticipation. And wrap it too.'

'You're very romantic,' she said.

He laughed. 'I try.'

She slipped the ribbon off and eased the painting out of its wrapping. 'Brother Fox,' she whispered.

'Or one of his close relatives,' said Jamie. 'Perhaps his grandfather.'

She looked at the painting more closely. Jamie was beside her, looking over her shoulder; she felt his breath against her neck, and every nerve ending down her spine seemed to tingle. The fox looked back at her; at the centre of his eyes a cleverly positioned tiny spot of white paint was light from the sky, reflected back towards the onlooker. How does an artist capture that electric moment of life, she asked herself, render it permanent in oils? 'How does he do it?' she said, half to herself, half to Jamie. 'How does he manage to make him . . . make him look so much like a fox?'

'He's very real, isn't he?' said Jamie. He reached forward to touch the painting with a forefinger. She saw the brown of his skin, so dear to her; he did not need the sun, as Cat did. Jamie's face, his hands, were a natural light brown, his Mediterranean colouring.

'You're touching him,' she said. 'I half expect him to turn round and nip you. But, look, he's quite unconcerned.'

She turned to Jamie, faced him. He was looking into her eyes, smiling. He bent slightly, for he was taller than Isabel, and kissed her, first on the cheek, then on the lips. He put his arms about her shoulders; his hands were warm against her. She let the painting slip from her fingers, but it was not damaged, as it fell on the cushion of the chair, face up, Brother Fox still staring at them, unperturbed.

They went to the Café St Honoré, a small French restaurant off Thistle Street. It was a favourite of Isabel's; intimate, but not so intimate as to inflict upon one the conversations of those at neighbouring tables. A perfect size, thought Isabel, mirroring the size of Edinburgh itself.

'I should not like to be completely anonymous,' Isabel remarked, looking about her. 'Imagine living somewhere like Tokyo, with twelve million people, or however many it is.'

'Perhaps Tokyo isn't as anonymous as it seems if one's Japanese. I suspect that people who live there don't feel all that anonymous. And what about London or New York? Are they all that anonymous? At least for the locals?'

Isabel thought about this. 'No, you're probably right. We carve out our little villages, even in big cities. There's our little village up in Merchiston. And Cat's village in the New Town.'

'Exactly,' said Jamie, picking up the menu which a waiter had placed before him. 'And when I walk through town, I usually see at least one of my pupils. Or the mother of one of them.' He paused, and smiled at a memory. 'I went into a bar the other day, you know, and there was one of the boys from the school, bold as brass. He's just sixteen, and I know which class he's in. And there he was in a bar.'

'Did he see you?'

'I think so. He looked away pretty sharply, and then I think he left. He was with somebody.'

'Boys will be . . .' began Isabel. Of course a sixteen-year-old boy would try to get into a bar if he thought he could get away with it; one should not be too surprised. But then she thought: What was Jamie doing in a bar? And when did he go to bars?

'Which bar?' she asked.

The question seemed to take him aback, and he hesitated before he answered. 'Oh, just a bar in George Street.'

'A wine bar?'

'That's what they call themselves.'

She looked at him. Had he been evasive? Or was it just her imagining things? She knew that she should not be possessive, but she could not help wondering whether he had gone into the bar by himself, or whether he had gone with somebody, or to meet somebody. People seldom went into bars by themselves unless they really needed a drink, or needed to kill time. Jamie needed neither – he was a light drinker, and he was always complaining about never having enough time. So he had gone in with somebody.

She looked down at the menu while she asked him. 'And you? Were you with somebody?'

She concentrated on the menu, reading the same line over and over, conscious of the fact that the question, in all its intrusiveness, lay unanswered on the tablecloth between them.

Then he replied: 'Sally. She used to play in the chamber orchestra. She doesn't any more, but I know her from that.'

Isabel did not look up. 'Have I met her?'

His voice was even, matter-of-fact. 'No.' He paused. 'You're wondering about her, aren't you?'

'Of course not,' Isabel lied. But her voice betrayed the truth;

she could not lie without her voice rising, breaking up, as if the words were clawed back and swallowed. They would never need a lie detector for her, she felt; the untruths would be so obvious to anyone with half an ear.

'Sally is going through a difficult time at the moment,' said Jamie. 'Her husband has been diagnosed with MS and they're taking it very badly. She needed a shoulder to cry on.'

Isabel looked up from the menu. 'I'm sorry,' she said. 'I'm very sorry.'

For a moment, Jamie looked at her with what might have been reproach, but then he looked down once more at the menu. 'You mustn't doubt me, Isabel,' he said quietly.

His words struck home. She reached out to take his hand. 'It's because I love you,' she said. 'I can't help that. I just do. I love you so much that I sit here thinking . . . Well, I just sit here thinking, What if he goes off with somebody else? What if he suddenly goes off me? I can't help it.'

He looked at her with astonishment. 'You think that?'

'That you'll leave me?'

'Yes. Do you really think that?'

She nodded, almost guiltily. Would he understand? Would any man understand that that is what so many women felt? And they felt it even if their husbands or boyfriends showed no inclination to go off with somebody else. They felt that because they would all have met some woman who would have said to them, I thought that I knew him so well, and now this. And in her case there was that additional worry that came with the difference in their ages. She had kept her looks, she was still attractive, but the years would show, eventually. And would he still find her appealing when that happened? It was the fear that so many women had, and one could not dismiss it, because in so many cases it proved to be well founded. The younger woman came along, and male biology asserted itself.

She had taken his hand; now he moved so that it was he who took hers. 'Isabel, listen. I'm the one who proposed to you. Remember? In Queen Street, after we had been at Lyon and Turnbull. I asked you to marry me then and you're the one who said no. So if anybody should do any worrying about the other leaving, then . . .'

They had never discussed that occasion; it had been left where it stood, an awkward memory. Now she wondered whether she should say, Ask me again. And this time, she would say yes, and she would put all doubt behind her. She had declined the first time because she had not wanted to take his freedom from him; but that had been purely because of the difference in their ages. Had the time come to stop worrying about that? Peter Stevenson had told her to stop thinking about it; perhaps he was right.

'All right, Isabel,' he had said. 'You have to stop worrying. We have. We thought when you began this that it might not last. But it has, hasn't it? And Charlie changes everything. So even if it's true that an age difference can lead to people drifting apart because they have different interests, that doesn't need to happen. All that the age difference might do is to put a little bit of extra strain on things. That's all.'

And perhaps this was exactly the strain that Peter had in mind. And she was the one who was creating it, by doubting Jamie, by turning him down when he wanted to cement things between them by asking her to marry him. She fulfilled the prophecy because she was doing precisely the thing that Jamie sometimes accused her of doing: thinking too much. Perhaps a philosopher should not think so much.

'I'm sorry. I'll stop. And if—' She was about to say: 'And if you want to ask me again to marry you, then ask me, and the answer will be different this time,' but before she could say this, Jamie interjected, 'Good. So let's talk about something else. Let's talk about Marcus Moncrieff.'

The moment had passed. Bad timing, thought Isabel, can change everything. There had been bad timing before – in 1708, to be precise, when the French ships carrying the Jacobites had arrived off Fife just a little bit too late for those ashore, who had melted away; but how absurd that she should think of that now.

Jamie, of course, had no idea that Isabel was thinking about the rising of 1708. 'I've been thinking about that poor man,' he went on. 'Are you going to be able to help him?'

She was not sure of her answer. She explained to Jamie about Stella's disclosure. Jamie thought it possible that Norrie Brown was responsible for what had happened, but he said, quite forcefully, that he did not think that it would have been out of personal animosity; the pharmaceutical company, in his view, was the likely villain.

'That lawyer who came to see you,' he said, 'David . . .'

'McLean.'

'Yes, him. He would have come to see you only if they had a real interest in stopping you. They wouldn't do it out of sympathy for Marcus Moncrieff. Why would they?'

Isabel nodded. 'So what do I do?'

'You go and see him. Tell him.'

'Who?'

'Marcus Moncrieff. Tell him that you suspect he was the innocent victim of a plan by the manufacturers of the drug to get the heat off them for a while. Those high figures suited them fine – it kept the drug on the market.'

'And then?'

Jamie shrugged. 'You bow out. You will have done what you set out to do – you will have come up with the information that he needs to clear his name. You can't do more than that.'

Isabel thought that Jamie was probably right. But she doubted whether she could really be said to have done very much; and it was unlikely that he did not now know about Norrie. Surely Stella would have told him that – although she would have put Norrie's intervention down to personal animosity. At least Isabel would be able to correct that impression.

She smiled at Jamie. 'You make it sound so simple,' she said. And then she was about to say, 'And as for marriage, well . . .' But Jamie, looking down at the menu again, said, 'What exactly is the difference between langoustines and crayfish?' and again the moment passed.

17

Jamie said to Isabel the next morning, 'You're going to go and see Marcus Moncrieff this morning. Remember?'

He was standing in his pyjamas in the kitchen, and Isabel, seeing that the pyjamas were immodest, said, 'Grace could come in, you know.'

Jamie hitched up the pyjama trousers, struggling with the cord, and Grace arrived, having let herself in silently. She looked away, but Jamie caught Isabel's eye.

'The bus was late again,' said Grace. 'And there was that man at the bus stop again. The peculiar one. The one who hands out leaflets about the second coming.'

Isabel rose from her seat. 'I'll go tomorrow,' she said, taking up the thread of her conversation with Jamie. 'I'll phone and ask them if they're going to be in.'

'Of course they're going to be in,' said Jamie. 'He never goes out. You told me.' He paused, looking at her knowingly. 'You're putting it off, aren't you, Isabel?'

'What?' asked Grace.

'A visit to an unhappy man,' said Jamie.

Isabel grimaced. 'This morning then?'

'I'll drive you,' said Jamie. 'Charlie and I will drive you, and then we can wait in the car on Johnston Terrace. Afterwards we can go somewhere. The Botanics, maybe.'

Isabel agreed. Jamie was right; she had been putting it off because she felt reluctant to face Marcus with bad news about his nephew. Should she go? Or should she just forget about the whole affair? She could do that; she was under no moral obligation to tell Marcus that he was the victim of deliberate manipulation by a pharmaceutical company. And yet, even as she thought this, she knew that she would not be able to rest until she had done all that she could to lighten his burden of shame. So she would go; she had to.

Charlie was still sleeping, and it was not until ten-thirty that they were in the green Swedish car and ready to leave. Grace had hinted broadly that she would be quite happy to look after Charlie and that he would surely enjoy himself more at home.

'I don't think so,' said Jamie.

Grace looked at him reproachfully. 'Being cooped up in the car—' she began.

'I don't think so,' Jamie said again. 'Thank you anyway, Grace.'

Outside, Isabel whispered, 'Well done!'

'He's my son,' said Jamie.

Isabel nodded her agreement. Grace meant well, but she had a tendency to assume that she knew best about most things, including Charlie's welfare. She felt proud of Jamie for sticking up for himself; she wanted him to do that, to be more assertive – within limits, of course.

'It's a very effective thing to say,' she remarked as they loaded Charlie into his car seat. '"I don't think so." It has a magisterial quality to it. I don't think so. And that's the end of the matter.'

'My mother used to say "argument over" a lot,' said Jamie. 'Sometimes she'd say it before we had the chance to open our mouths. "Argument over." And that was that.'

Isabel went round to the passenger side of the car and opened the door. Jamie very rarely spoke about his family. His parents, she understood, were divorced, and his mother had left Scotland to live in London with a new husband, whom Jamie did not get on with. His father had left the country altogether and lived in Spain. There had been a sister, who had married a naval officer, but he said that he very rarely heard from her.

'Do you miss them?' she had once asked.

He had replied, 'No. Not really. We've all grown apart, I suppose.' And then he had changed the subject, and she had seen this as a sign that he did not want to talk more about it. But it was also for her a confirmation that he did miss them.

'Will you say "argument over" to Charlie, do you think?' she asked.

He was dismissive. 'Of course not.'

Isabel reached for her seat belt and draped it over her shoulder. The green Swedish car was a safe car, but Swedish glass made the same impression on the human head as any lesser glass. 'And yet people do tend to say the things that their parents said, don't they? We become our parents, you know. We think that we never will, but we do. We start talking like them, acting like them, holding the same views that they held, no matter how much we think that we don't.' Her sainted American mother had been a model to her, and she would willingly have emulated her – except perhaps for her little failing, her affair.

Jamie thought about this as he slipped the key into the ignition. 'Do we? No, I don't think we do.' And then he added, 'Argument over.'

Isabel had telephoned ahead, and Stella was expecting her.

'I told him,' she said, as she met Isabel at the door.

'That I was coming?'

Stella shook her head. 'No. I told him that I thought that Norrie was responsible. That he had changed the figures.'

Isabel raised an eyebrow. 'And what did he say to that?'

Stella looked pained. 'He went off the deep end. He told me that it was absolute nonsense. He said that Norrie had never had any interest in the place up north and that the whole idea was ridiculous.' She sighed. 'He just refused to listen to what I had to say. He refused point-blank.'

Isabel frowned. 'Well, I can't imagine that he's going to take it from me, either.'

'Please try,' said Stella. 'At least try. Even if he won't listen to me, then he might pay attention to somebody who's more or less a stranger. He can hardly be as rude to you as he was to me.'

'I'll try,' said Isabel. But she felt it was hopeless. All the evidence she had to back up her theory that Norrie and the drug manufacturers had acted together was her visit from David McLean – and that was hardly evidence. And then there was the question of Marcus's depression. People in a state of depression often did not listen, being so caught up in their misery, their preoccupations. Marcus was suddenly not going to become open, become rational, just because of a few facts put before him by Isabel.

She followed Stella through to the drawing room with the wide window. Marcus was sitting exactly where he had been when she had last visited him; it was as if he had not moved at all. And he had probably moved very little. Perhaps he slept in that chair, she thought. Day in, day out, he sat there, virtually immobile. If this was shame, or guilt, then it was as vivid an instance of it as one might imagine.

'Isabel Dalhousie has come to see you,' announced Stella in a loud voice. She spoke as if she was addressing a child, or someone hard of hearing.

Marcus Moncrieff looked up and stared at Isabel. His expression was flat, but for a moment there was a flicker of a smile, a wan smile, produced, thought Isabel, through great effort. 'Miss Dalhousie? Good morning.' It was said without enthusiasm, but Isabel thought the instinctive good manners of the Edinburgh doctor had not deserted him. Some of that was still there – fragments of personality surviving the onslaught of the clinical depression.

He tried to rise to his feet out of politeness, but Stella put a hand on his shoulder and gently pressed him back into his chair. 'She won't mind if you don't get up,' she said. 'She can sit here.'

She gestured to a chair in front of the window. Isabel shook hands with Marcus before she sat down opposite him. She glanced through the window; down below, far below, the buses crawled along Princes Street; flags fluttered from the top of the Scottish National Gallery, a Union flag and a Scottish saltire. Beyond the gallery, the curious spire of the Scott Monument, blackened by ancient soot, poked at the sky. Walter Scott in his chair looking upon a street that would be recognisable to him in some ways even today, but in others so alien; a street taken over by strangers.

Marcus interrupted her thoughts. 'You've come to see me

about this business of my nephew,' he said. 'Or I assume that's what you've come about.'

Isabel fixed him in the eye. 'Yes. I have.'

He turned away, to face the window; he was not looking at the city below, but at the sky somewhere over Fife. 'Norrie had nothing to do with it. I've told Stella. It had absolutely nothing to do with him.' He turned to face her. 'I give you my word on that, you know. Nothing to do with it.' He paused. 'How do I make you believe that? What does it take?'

Nothing more than you are doing at the moment, thought Isabel. Nothing more than the truth that you are so evidently telling me. He was not lying; she could tell that from his demeanour. And she made her decision.

'I believe you,' she said. 'All right, let's say that Norrie had nothing to do with it. But that doesn't mean that there might not have been others who deliberately altered that data. People who stood to gain from it.'

'Such as?' he snapped.

'The people who made the drugs. The pharmaceutical company.'

He looked at her almost with pity. 'Are you one of those people who believe the worst of pharmaceutical companies? Who thinks that everything they do – everything – is selfish, exploitative, wicked? Is that what you really believe?'

She defended herself. 'No, I'm not one of those people, as you put it. But you can't deny that some pharmaceutical companies have played fast and loose with people on occasion. Have tried to get doctors to prescribe useless or marginally useful drugs. Who have charged too much. Who have sometimes concealed evidence that doesn't suit them. You can't deny that.'

215

'Sometimes,' he said, begrudgingly. 'Sometimes. But you're always going to get some rotten apples. That's human nature. They're probably no better nor worse than any other businesses. It's called capitalism, Miss Dalhousie. But the real point, surely, is that they invent and make drugs that save lives. Look at AIDS. How long ago was that a sure and certain death sentence? And now? Something you can live with for years and years. And who do we thank for that? The pharmaceutical companies who produce the ARVs. That's who.'

He looked at her triumphantly, as if challenging her to refute the irrefutable. Isabel merely nodded. 'Of course. But what if your case was one where the bad apples were at work? How would you feel if I were to demonstrate to you that they had a role in distorting those figures? And then you took the blame?'

For a while he said nothing. She watched him, and she thought that he looked like a man in the grip of some awful internal struggle. And when he spoke, it became clear that he was.

'You could never demonstrate that to me,' he said. 'For a very simple reason. I did it.'

'You told me that already. You admitted that you failed to check the results. You told me that when we first met.'

He became agitated. 'Oh no, I didn't tell you. I didn't tell you what I did.' He stopped, closed his eyes and turned away, so that she might not see his face. His hands, Isabel saw, were shaking. 'I altered the figures myself.' There was a pause. Had she heard correctly? The words were like the stones of a wall – physical things. And then, 'The original reports from the lab indicated relatively small overdoses. I changed them and made it seem that the overdoses had been massive. I did it, and it was

216

very easy. I just tore up the original forms and filled in new ones. Simple.'

He spoke slowly and clearly, enunciating each word. The shock that Isabel felt on hearing this did not stop her from watching his face as he spoke. It was a face that reflected pain in every word of the confession. And again she realised that he was telling the truth.

She was silent for a time after he had finished. Then she said, quite gently, 'Why did you do it, Dr Moncrieff?'

He answered quickly. 'Because I believed it was the right thing to do.'

'How could it be? How could it be right to mislead people on this?'

He sat back in his chair and opened his eyes. 'Because I really believed in the drug. I thought that the reaction in each case was probably triggered by something that had nothing to do with the drug – especially in the case of the drug addict. They take God knows how many different things. I thought that those two cases were completely freak events: one caused by a whole cocktail of stuff which an addict had taken; another caused by a nurse who got things dramatically wrong, or a patient who secretly stuffed himself with pills. I thought the drug was completely safe and that this was just a nonsense that would set us all back five years. People were dying, remember. I wanted to stop that. That drug was our best hope and the last thing we wanted was a scare over it. We're never . . .' He seemed to struggle to find the right words. 'We're never going to get anywhere if we allow this absurd safety culture to inhibit us. You have to take some risks to get somewhere. You just have to. But try telling that to the assorted bureaucrats and lawyers and ethics people, not one of whom, may I say, has ever done anything but inhibit new treatments. Try getting through to that bunch. What about Lister?' He pointed out of the window, in the direction of the Queen Street drawing room where Lister and his friends had taken chloroform at the dining-room table. 'Would Lister ever have been allowed to self-experiment like that today?' He laughed. 'You can bet your bottom dollar he would not. Health and safety. Informed consent. All that claptrap, all while people are dying.'

He stopped and looked at Isabel. 'So there you have it,' he said. 'I did it because I thought I knew best. And then . . . then that poor man died.'

'You didn't want that,' said Isabel.

'Didn't want it? Of course I didn't want it. But I'm responsible for it. If I had blown the whistle on the drug, then it wouldn't have happened. So what do you want me to say, Miss Dalhousie? That I was wrong? Right, I've said it. I was wrong. I was proud. I thought I knew best.'

They sat in silence. It was a curious silence, one that neither felt he or she needed to bring to an end. It was a silence that comes when the worst has been said and there is nothing more to be added.

But Isabel said to herself: If he thought there was no risk, then where exactly was the wrongdoing – in the moral sense? He had not taken a deliberate risk, because a deliberate risk implies knowledge that harm might materialise; he thought that what he did was safe. It was not. He had been arrogant in thinking that he knew better than those who had set in place all the precautions that protected patients. They were right; he was wrong. But he had thought it was the other way round.

'So what now?' he suddenly said.

Isabel said nothing. She was still thinking.

'So you report me?'

She shook her head. 'No. I don't report you.'

He seemed surprised. 'Why? Don't I deserve it?'

'I think that you've already been punished,' she said. 'You resigned. You lost your position – and your reputation. You feel all this shame.' She paused, watching him, watching the effect of her words. 'And anyway, if I reported you, or if I urged you to report yourself, it would merely lead to more proceedings against you. You'd be struck off the medical register. And I'm afraid that you would kill yourself.'

He said nothing. He did nothing to confirm or deny what she had said, and that convinced her that she was right. The question over which this man ponders, she thought, sitting in that chair of his, is whether to kill himself.

'I don't think that you could take any more shaming, could you?'

He moved his head slightly but it was assent.

'And if you kill yourself, then what purpose does that serve? Stella is left behind. Her life is ruined. And we all lose a man who had a good few useful years ahead of him. So – in my view – there's no point at all in more punishment. There's such a thing as a just measure of punishment, and I think you've had it.'

He watched her closely. 'You don't think that I'm responsible for that man's death?'

'No,' said Isabel. 'On balance, I don't. Not in any sense that really counts. And I think that because you had no idea that what you did could kill somebody. In your . . . your arrogance, you thought that you knew best whether it was safe to do what you did. You betrayed your training, your oath, everything; but you didn't think that it would kill anybody.'

'I didn't,' he said quietly. 'I really didn't.'

'No,' said Isabel. 'And I believe you.' She hesitated. He was watching her, willing her to say something; but what?

'What do you think you can do now to make up for all this?' she said.

He looked perplexed. 'I don't see what I can do.'

'Couldn't you get back into medicine?' she asked. 'Not here, obviously. But somewhere where they might be glad of your services. Somewhere where they really need you?'

He sat quite still. 'I never thought . . .'

'No,' she said. 'But why don't you think about it now? Why don't you set yourself a penance? Penance comes in different forms – not just the mortification of the transgressor. It comes in doing something good for somebody else.' It was ancient language; people did not set themselves penances any more. But did that mean that penance was no longer needed? Here, she thought, is a case which disproves that. And it disproves, too, the proposition that I am capable of finding things out. I'm not. I get everything wrong.

She made to leave him, and he rose to his feet. There had been crumbs of food on his jacket, and they fell to the ground like tiny hailstones. He called for Stella, and began to walk with Isabel.

'Thank you,' he said.

'You don't have to thank me,' she said. 'I found nothing out, and what I did find out I got wrong.'

He smiled. This time it was not weak, nor was it forced. 'But you gave me the chance to confess,' he said.

'I have no power to forgive. I am not a priest.'

'It is too late for a priest in my case,' he said. 'I lost that comfort a long time ago.'

'Then you have to make do as best you can.'

He nodded. 'You've told me what to do,' he said.

She wondered whether he would do it.

Jamie and Charlie were waiting for her in Johnston Terrace. Charlie stared up at her from the padded cocoon of his travel seat. But he looked away quickly, distracted by a glint of sun on a silver door handle within the car.

'So what happened?' asked Jamie.

'I found out that I was completely wrong,' said Isabel. 'And you were too.'

It reassured her that she could embrace Jamie in her error. 'I'm a hopeless sleuth,' she said. 'I really am.' She thought, though, that perhaps that did not matter; she had a vague sense of having just saved a life, although she was not sure exactly how she had reached that point, and of course one does not think of such things. The moral account book, wherever it is – in some distant metaphysical databank, or just in the heart – should never be contemplated, nor dwelt upon.

Jamie leaned over and kissed her lightly on the cheek. He felt so fond of her; he loved her so, this interfering woman, this flawed but noble soul. 'You always seem to sort things out,' he said. 'Even if you get it all wrong, you sort things out.'

'You can do the right thing for the wrong reason, I suppose,' said Isabel. 'Eliot says something about that, doesn't he?'

'He might,' said Jamie. 'He said all sorts of things.'

Isabel laughed. 'Name one.'

It was a direct challenge. '*A cold coming we had of it,*' said Jamie.

'*Just the worst time of the year for a journey,*' continued Isabel, '*And such a journey.*'

Jamie laughed. '*I will show you fear in a handful of dust.* And that's all the Eliot I know. Remember, I'm just a musician.'

Isabel needed only a second or two to remember the lines that followed. '*Frisch weht der Wind,*' she said. '*Der Heimat zu / Mein irisch Kind / Wo weilest du?*' Fresh wafts the wind to the Homeland/My Irish child/Where do you linger?

Charlie started to cry. He had had quite enough of this.

'*Mein scottische Kind,*' said Isabel. '*Warum weinest du?*' My Scottish child – why do you weep?

'That will only make him worse,' said Jamie.

It did.

He addressed Charlie in Scots. 'Whisht now, bairn. Dinnae greet.' Hush, child. Don't cry.

Charlie was calmed.

'You see?' said Jamie.

They drove off, in the green Swedish car, with the castle towering above them, and above that a sky from which the clouds had drawn back to reveal an attenuated blue, cold and pure.

18

Saturday came, Isabel's favourite day, and Jamie's too – if there was no concert that evening. And that Saturday there was none, leaving him free to cook dinner, which he liked to do over the weekends. Charlie, for whom one day was very much the same as another, awoke early; he was ready for breakfast shortly after half past five, disturbed, perhaps, by the birds who had loud territorial business on a tree outside his window. Jamie heard him and slipped out of bed, telling Isabel that she could have a lie-in. 'As long as you like,' he muttered drowsily. 'I'll take him down to the canal and then . . .'

That was as much as she heard before she drifted back to sleep, and when she finally got out of bed at nine, the house was empty. The canal towpath was a good place to push Charlie in the new three-wheeled jogging pushchair that they had recently acquired; they could go for miles, to Ratho if they wished, and beyond. Isabel went downstairs in her dressing gown and opened the shutters in her study. The morning light on that side of the house was bright, and a band of it cut, butter-yellow, through the room, showing the particles of dust in their swirling dance. The air was not empty, she thought – nothing was.

The postman had come. He arrived early on Saturdays and considerately refrained from ringing the bell when he had a parcel, leaving it discreetly propped up against the door. 'Your philosophy stuff,' he said of the bundles of manuscripts and proofs that found their way to her door. 'Do you think I'd understand any of it? I doubt it.'

'You'd understand philosophy perfectly well, Billy,' she said. 'Everybody's a philosopher. You have views, don't you?'

'Aye, I have my views.'

'Well, there you are then: you do philosophy. Would you like a copy of my journal – the philosophy magazine I edit? I can give you one.'

'No, thank you.' And then, 'That's very kind of you, Isabel, but no, thank you.'

On that morning, though, there were no parcels, but there were several large envelopes which were *Review* business, accompanied by a fistful of bills and a couple of personal letters. One of these letters was from an old school friend who lived in Cheltenham and wrote at irregular intervals to share with Isabel her complaints about her husband, a philanderer whom she perversely refused to leave. Isabel opened this letter with the usual heart-sinking feeling that her friend's letters triggered.

I'm furious with Robert. He imagines that I don't see a thing, but I see it all – he's so transparent. He seems to be smitten with a dreadful blowsy woman who runs a small spaghetti restaurant down here. That's all she cooks: spaghetti. In these days of more sophisticated tastes you'd think that the customers would want something a little bit more adventurous, but no, it's just spaghetti. He went to Italy with her. He told me – *promised* me – that he was going to Rome on business, but what do I find in his shirt pocket when he comes back? Two boarding passes to Naples, one in his name and one in the name of La Spaghetti. And then he denied it. He said he had picked up another passenger's boarding pass which he had found on the side of the basin in the plane's loo. He had meant to hand it in, but forgot to so do. That's what he said. Can you believe it, Isabel? Can you? That's an excuse on a par with the famous *The dog ate my homework*, isn't it?'

It was a weak excuse, thought Isabel, but what if it were true? There were excuses that seemed extremely implausible, but which were actually true. There were, she imagined, dogs who did eat homework. It's the sort of thing that a terrier might do; they often worried away at things they found lying around the house, and why not homework? She had known of a dog who had, in a single afternoon, polished off a box of chocolates (potentially fatal to dogs) and a set of stereo headphones. Such things happened. People did find boarding passes on planes and put them in their pockets with the best of intentions. And if one had such an excuse, and if it was genuine, then how must it feel not to be believed? But of course she did not believe him in this case.

She laid her friend's letter aside. The husband would continue to philander and his wife would continue to complain about him. But they would stay together in their unhappiness, as people did. They remained. They endured.

The second letter was altogether more cheerful. Her psychiatrist friend, Richard Latcham, had found an article in a psychiatric journal which he thought might interest her. He had photocopied it and sent it to her. She paged through it: 'The Psychopath and His Childhood'. Psychopathy starts very early, wrote the author. At six or seven, the psychopathic die is probably cast. There then followed several examples of well-known psychopaths: a famous newspaper proprietor, an actor, Lawrence of Arabia. There were photographs of them as boys, small boys, in shorts. Lawrence already looked cold; the newspaper proprietor already avaricious; the actor preternaturally vain and self-centred.

Isabel put the article down on a table and turned to Richard's letter. 'The enclosed should interest you. V. perceptive, I thought. And it goes to show how *they're all around us* – psychopaths, Isabel: watch out.'

And she suddenly thought: Marcus Moncrieff? He had been utterly indifferent to the rules of his own calling; he had been so proud. But he felt guilt – crippling, overwhelming guilt – and a psychopath would not have felt that. He would have simply got on with things; found something else. He would not have tortured himself over the death of the man in Glasgow.

She returned to Richard's letter. He moved on from psychopaths and began to tell her about a dinner he had been to in Newmarket.

I drove over there in the Bristol. That's the one you loved – remember it? It was the annual dinner of the Newmarket Society for the Apprehension of Felons and the Prevention of Crime. Yes, that's what it really is called. It was founded in the nineteenth century and has just continued, although it doesn't do anything about apprehending felons or preventing crime any more. A lot of these societies forget about their original purpose, but still enjoy an annual dinner. Anyway, there I was with this group of lawyers and local businessmen and so on, and one of the committee members got up to say grace, as he always does each year: a mushroom-compost manufacturer.

He's on the committee. And the grace he says is this: 'They're under starter's orders . . . and they're off.' And then he sits down. That's what I like about this country, Isabel. It's so utterly eccentric, so unpredictable.

Isabel looked at her watch. She had a feeling that Jamie and Charlie would be out for some time yet. Jamie sometimes walked down to his flat with Charlie to check up on mail; he might do that today. And once he was down there in Stockbridge, he often dropped into the Patisserie Florentin for breakfast and conversation with whoever might be there. Other fathers went there, he said, and talked while their children played about their feet. New men, of course, and to be encouraged.

She dressed, scribbled a note for Jamie should he come back early, and left for Bruntsfield. Cat had been back for a full week now, and although she had intended to drop in to see her, Isabel had not done so. Part of her hankered after the bustle of the delicatessen and would have traded her editor's chair for the busy cheese counter. But another part knew that she was a philosopher at heart; that this is what she did, what she was most fulfilled doing. Perhaps the two could somehow be combined. There were philosophers' cafés, of course, where people met and discussed philosophical issues. Isabel's friend in Vancouver told her they were popular there and suggested that she set up one in Edinburgh. Perhaps a philosophers' delicatessen, especially if Cat lost interest in the business and went off to Sri Lanka: Cheese and Philosophy, a place where people might come in, sample and buy cheese, and then join a discussion group. Eddie could assist, but would have to be taught the rudiments of philosophy first; just enough to prevent his letting slip that he thought Aristotle was a cheese. It could work, she thought, but it would have to join the list of things she would like to do one day, if she had time. And there never would be time now. Now there was Charlie, and Jamie, and the *Review*, for which she alone was responsible. As Charlie grew up there would be all his interests to take into account: his friends, his dance class . . . She stopped herself. Would Charlie dance? Why had she thought he would? She must be careful. Charlie was a boy – an entirely different creature from herself. She must open herself to the things that Charlie might be interested in as a boy: football, for example. And football left Isabel cold; she simply could not understand where the appeal lay in vying for the possession of a leather ball and kicking it. Did men *need* to kick things? She would ask Jamie. She had never seen him kick anything, but perhaps he felt – in some deep, entirely masculine part of himself – the urge to kick something.

When she arrived at the delicatessen there were only two customers, one at the counter, being served by Eddie, the other seated, a newspaper open in front of him and a steaming cappuccino beside it. Isabel nodded to Eddie, who smiled at her and made a sipping motion with a hand. Would she like coffee? She nodded and made her way across the shop towards the half-open door of Cat's office.

Cat was at her desk, carefully removing the sticking tape from round the top of a tin of sugared almonds. She glanced up when Isabel appeared.

'These have passed their sell-by date,' she said. 'But I'm sure that they're fine. I'm just checking.'

Isabel said nothing. She did not approve, but said nothing.

'Eddie is going to make me a cappuccino,' she said. 'Will you join me?'

Cat struggled with the tape, which kept sticking to her fingers. 'What's it like out there?' she asked.

228

'Not very busy,' said Isabel. 'Rather quiet, in fact. We were pretty busy last Saturday.'

'Eddie told me,' said Cat. 'And thank you. I gather you were both worked pretty hard.'

Isabel was about to say something, but did not. She had been about to say, 'And all for no pay!' But she thought, correctly, it would not help. She did not need the money, which is what Cat would think. So she said nothing.

Cat joined her at the table a few minutes later as Eddie brought them both their coffee. Eddie smiled at Isabel again.

'How's . . .' Isabel wanted to ask after Eddie's girlfriend, but found that she could not remember her name. In fact, she thought that Eddie had never told her, and she could hardly say, How's that girl in black? or How's that girl with the piercings?

'Virginia?' volunteered Eddie.

It seemed an inappropriate name to Isabel, but she nodded.

'History,' said Eddie. And smiled.

Both Isabel and Cat were taken aback. Cat glanced at Isabel, an eyebrow raised. 'It's over?' she asked.

'Yup,' said Eddie. 'She's history.'

'You don't seem too upset,' Isabel ventured.

'Cried my eyes out,' Eddie replied. 'For an hour maybe. Not any more.'

He left them. Cat smiled. 'It's different,' she whispered. 'It's just different.'

'He seems pleased,' said Isabel.

'Of course he'll be pleased,' Cat snapped. 'They're not into commitment, his age group.'

Isabel sipped at her cappuccino. Cat was hardly one to talk about commitment, she thought, with her record.

'Have you started to look for your new manager yet?' she asked.

Cat looked out of the window. 'No. In fact, I don't think I will.'

Isabel hesitated.

'There's a change of plan,' said Cat. 'I've decided not to go out to Sri Lanka.'

'Not at all?'

'Well, I might visit it again sometime. I liked it. But not for a while.'

Isabel was not sure whether she should ask the question she was burning to ask. Simon. Cat looked at her astutely; the question did not need to be asked.

'Simon and I have parted company,' she said. 'It didn't work. Long-distance relationships . . .'

Isabel reached out and touched Cat. 'I'm sorry.' She was. Cat needed love and affection and got instead passing and unsatisfactory romance, time after time. But it was her fault – if fault came into it. She looked in the wrong place, for the wrong men, and applied the wrong criteria. That sort of thing, of course, was very rarely something for which a person could be blamed. It was a character defect of the sort which we can rarely do anything about. In sexual matters, we dance to a tune which was composed for us a long time ago, by somebody else, by our parents perhaps, or by biology. Cat's father, Isabel's brother, was a remote, handsome man. Every single one of Cat's boyfriends had struck Isabel as being in some way remote. And every one of them was good-looking in a particular way – the way of Isabel's brother at that age. Simon, she was sure, would have been like that.

She suddenly asked: 'You don't have a photograph of him, do you?'

Cat looked at her in astonishment. 'Why?'

'I'm curious. That's all. I've seen most of your boyfriends. But not him.'

Cat shrugged. 'I've got some photos from Sri Lanka through there in the office. He'll be in some of them.'

'Please let me see.'

'I suppose so. If you really want to.'

She rose and disappeared into her office, to reappear a few minutes later with a small folder of photographs. 'Look at the shots of Galle,' she said. 'It'll make you want to go there.'

Isabel opened the folder and took out the photographs. On the top was a picture of a small island, just a few yards out to sea. The island was topped by a white villa, a tattered flag flying limply from the high point of its roof.

Cat looked over Isabel's shoulder. 'Taprobane Island,' she said. 'We went there for lunch with a friend. He lives there. It's the most wonderful place.'

'And here?' asked Isabel.

There was a group of ten or twelve people on a beach. A highly coloured fishing boat was drawn up on the sand behind them. 'That was further down the coast. We went there before we went to a tea plantation – the place where I bought that white tea I gave you. Have you tried it yet?'

'Not yet,' muttered Isabel. She was looking at the group of people. Cat was there, and she was standing next to a man, who had an arm around her. But even without that, Isabel could tell.

'That's him, isn't it? That's Simon?'

Cat glanced at the photograph, and looked away again quickly. 'Yes.'

'He's . . . so good-looking.' She spoke quietly. 'And he looks so like my brother. Your father. Isn't that strange?'

She said nothing else, but moved on to the next photograph.

The tea estate. 'That was where they dried the tea. Over there,' said Cat. 'And do you see that man? That one? He showed us round. Tea was his life.'

But she spoke as one who was thinking of something else. Isabel could tell that, and she wondered whether she had planted the seed of something that might help Cat; she hoped that she had. Some women searched for their fathers; some men searched for their mothers. Sometimes it was better to search for neither. But she could never tell Cat that; not directly.

She had a few purchases to make in Bruntsfield, and she went directly from the delicatessen to the fish shop at Holy Corner. She wanted langoustines, and she was pleased to see that there were some, neatly arranged on a marble slab in the window, along with squid and wild salmon. While the fishmonger selected them for her, placing them on a piece of greaseproof paper, she asked him about how they differed from crayfish. 'Langoustines are saltwater decapods,' he said. 'Decapods. Nice word, isn't it, Isabel? And crayfish, which are crawfish over the Pond, are freshwater decapods. But, if you're in France, then prawns are called langoustines. As an act of charity towards the humble prawns, I think. To promote them a bit.'

It was an entirely satisfactory conversation. Isabel liked talking to people who knew their subject, and the fishmonger knew all about fish. Many people in shops did not know what they were talking about, she thought. They just sold things; the fishmonger, and people like him, believed in things.

She left the fish shop and wandered down to the newsagent near the post office. She would buy a paper – perhaps two – and a couple of magazines. *Scottish Field*, perhaps, because it was so full of comforting things: dogs, wildlife, lochs, glens – an unchanging Scotland that started just a mile or two from where she was standing, where the Pentland Hills swept down to the edge of the city. Then, armed with her purchases, she would go back to the house and think about lunch. She was happy.

She sauntered back. The morning was comfortable – warm enough for the time of the year – and the sky was clear. A few gulls, circling overhead, mewled in the wind, and then glided away, disturbed, perhaps, by the sudden appearance of a small formation of geese heading west. The geese were flying low for some reason and she heard the muffled sound of their pinions on the air, that slight thumping sound, punctuated by the calls of the leader. She stood still for a moment, half way down Merchiston Crescent, and watched them pass overhead. Within hours they would be in the Hebrides, at the very edge of Europe, where they would land on the *machair*, the sweet pastures of the islands.

Jamie was already at home when she arrived. Charlie had slept for much of his outing and was wide awake now. Isabel changed him, and took off his McPherson tartan rompers in favour of a loose white tee-shirt, more suitable for the warmth of the day.

'We can sit outside,' she said. 'A bit later on I'll make a picnic lunch.'

It had rained the previous day, and although the grass had dried out in the morning sun, the earth was still wet. Jamie decided that he would replant the bulbs that Brother Fox had dug up again. And there were several shrubs that Isabel had ordered from a horticultural catalogue waiting to be planted.

She sat on the blanket, a book beside her, but she did not read. She played with Charlie. He had a small stuffed fox that Jamie had bought him. He loved it.

Jamie worked in the garden for an hour or so and then rejoined them on the rug. Charlie was drowsy now, and had been put, with a feeding cup, on an infant deck chair that rocked gently backwards and forwards. He would drop off to sleep, the beak of the feeding cup still in his mouth.

Isabel looked at Jamie. 'You're covered in mud,' she said. 'Look, stand up, and I'll brush it off you.'

She stood beside him. There was mud upon the knees of his trousers, where he had been kneeling. She brushed it off. 'Mud and Saturdays go well together,' he said.

'Yes,' she said. 'They do.'

She examined his shirt; there were small patches of mud on the sleeves. She brushed these off too, gently, with love.

Brother Fox, unseen, watched them from the shadows of a rhododendron bush. There were the red flowers of the bush above him, and below him the muddy earth in which he made his burrow, his sanctuary. When Isabel and Jamie went inside, briefly, to get the things for lunch, he padded out across the grass and sniffed gently at the sleeping child. Then he turned away and pressed his wet black nose against the stuffed fox. It smelt of milk. Brother Fox took it in his jaws and began to carry it across the lawn. But then, when a sound came from within the house, he dropped the soft toy in the middle of the lawn and slunk back into the shadows.

'How did that happen?' asked Jamie.

Isabel put a tray down on the ground and looked at Charlie, still asleep. She did not answer the question because she was not in any mood to solve the problems of others, and all she wanted to say was 'I am so very happy.' Which she did; and she was.